Shameless

MICHELLE HEARD

TABLE OF CONTENTS

Dedication

Laura, Leeann, Kelly, Kristine & Morgan.
This one's for you.

Hummingbirds' wings create the infinity symbol when in flight. They represent endurance, adaptability, and also bring playfulness and joy to life.

Chapter 1

Evie

Seventeen years old...

Having done my chores for the day, I drag my tired body to the bedroom I share with Sandra and Wendy. Sandra will be back from work at three am, and Wendy is already fast asleep. Sandra is two weeks older than me and started working last week when she turned eighteen. She's moving to *Moonlight Ranch* tomorrow.

Just thinking about what the future holds for me sends a shiver of disgust rippling through me. I only have one week left before I have to start working at that hellhole, as well.

Eric and Charlotte are cunning and deceitful. They've mastered the art of fooling welfare services whenever they come to do an inspection. The house is always neat, and they make sure that no *business* takes place on the premises. Everything happens at the ranch, and only at night. During the day, it functions as just another ordinary cattle ranch. Most of the boys who come to live here are lucky because they get to work on the ranch during the day. Although, the attractive ones get handpicked by Charlotte to work at night alongside all the girls.

From the outside, everything looks normal. Eric and Charlotte regularly donate and are respected by the community. I've learned that money can buy a lot of things.

Hell, they even had me fooled when I first came to live with them. I thought I was one of the lucky ones when I got placed with the Williams family. I was only thirteen and still held onto the hope that I would find a family I could call my own.

Instead of a family, I found monsters who use us for cheap labor, and once you turn eighteen, you're forced to become a sex worker.

Eric and Charlotte can sweet-talk anyone into believing they're saints. They're smart, never letting their perverted clients touch any of the underage girls. But once we turn eighteen, all bets are off. You either start working for them, or you're out on the cold street without a second thought. It still surprises me how many girls choose to stay.

Even though I'm tired, I can't fall asleep. Since Sandra starting working, I've been spending my nights worrying about my eighteenth birthday.

I'm planning to run away. It's all I can do to save myself from a life as a prostitute. I shudder with revulsion, just thinking about some perverted old man touching me.

So far, I've managed to hide some food behind the washing machine. Once I'm living on the street, I know the food won't last long, but right now, my biggest concern is where I'll live. I'm scared to death of being homeless, but it's nothing compared to the fear of having countless men use my body any way they want to for the rest of my life.

I have no other choice but to run away.

Feeling hopeless and terrified of what my future holds in store for me, I curl into a small bundle.

Alienated. It's the only word that describes how I feel. Unloved and disregarded by life, I wonder why I was born if I'm meant to be snubbed by everyone? People either look right through me or glare at me with disdain.

During my first week on the streets, I was too scared to even sleep. Every person who crossed my path was a potential threat. Up until a few weeks ago, being raped was my biggest fear.

I was wrong.

Loneliness has become my greatest fear by far. I was never close to any of the other children who were taken in by Eric and Charlotte, but at least I wasn't alone while I lived there.

There's not a single person who cares about me. I could disappear from the face of the planet, and no one would notice.

I might as well not exist.

The realization is devastating. When I least expect it, it hits me with one crippling blow after another. The thought will wake me minutes after I've drifted off, or slam into me while I'm walking down the street.

The only reminder I have that I'm alive is my aching stomach. I can't remember the last decent meal I ate. The food I stole before I ran away was taken on my second day out here. I had hidden it behind a dumpster while I was looking for work. When I returned to the alley where I thought I'd be able to stay until I managed to find a job, two men were going through my things, dividing it all amongst themselves. They were much bigger than me, and fearing for my life, I had no choice but to leave with only the bag I had with me.

Desperation shudders through me, and for a moment, I think about searching through the dumpsters near restaurants, but then I remember the beating I got when I accidentally trespassed on another homeless man's area. That's another thing I quickly learned. Deprivation makes savages of people. On the streets, you'll be ripped apart if you so much as look at another person.

I hunch forward, hugging my arms around my waist as I try and fight off the chill. I tried to sneak into the library's bathroom, but security caught me. I was thrown out with a harsh warning. It could've been worse. I was lucky they didn't have me arrested. I also tried to walk up and down the aisles of shops that stayed open during the night, but it became unbearable. Seeing all that food and not being able to eat any of it was pure torture.

I've thought about going back to Eric and Charlotte, but when I think of what I'll be going back to, I'd rather die. Being at the mercy of a pimp and his whore, I will only have two options. Either I get busy spreading my legs to earn my keep, or I leave.

I look up at the sign that reads *Double D's Cleaning Services*. Saying a silent prayer, I open the door and walk into the reception area. If I don't get a job soon, I don't know what I'll do. I'm reaching the point where I'm so desperate that I'll even take a job as a stripper.

Chapter 2

Rhett

Nineteen years old.

People say they love you, but what they actually mean is that they love how you make them feel about themselves, or what they can take from you.

That's the lesson I learned the day my parents died. If it weren't for Mr. Hayes, Mia and I would've had nowhere to go.

Our parents worked hard for the little we had. There wasn't a lot of money, but there was love. Fuck, we had the best parents. Not a day has gone by where I don't miss them.

Where I look like Dad, Mia is the spitting image of Mom. We both have black hair, but Mia got Mom's striking green eyes. My eyes are dark, sometimes brown and sometimes black, depending on my mood. My sister is my opposite. Where I'm big, she's small, which only brings out my protective side even more. There's nothing I won't do for Mia.

We had family who could've taken us in when our parents died, but Mia and I were nothing more than burdens to them. Our *family* couldn't afford to be saddled with us. That was until Mr. Hayes stepped in, and suddenly our so-called family was interested in us again. I'm so thankful for Mr. Hayes. Financially, we had everything our hearts could desire, and he was a fantastic father figure to me.

But Mia needed more than that. She needed a mother. I went from struggling through puberty to becoming Mia's protector overnight. I was no longer someone's son. Even though Mr. Hayes was the perfect father figure, I still had to become Mia's mother, father, and be her big brother all at the same time. It was easier for me to connect with Mr. Hayes than it was for Mia.

I'll never forget the day I realized just how badly Mia needed a mother.

I open my bedroom door and frown when I see Mia sitting on my bed. As she looks up at me, her chin starts to quiver.

"What's wrong?" I ask while shutting the door behind me.

She shakes her head and looks back down at her hands.

Taking a seat next to her, I duck my head lower, trying to catch her eyes. "I can't make it better if you don't tell me."

"It started today," she whispers as her tears start to fall.

"What started?"

She mumbles something I can't make out as sobs shudder through her tiny body.

"I didn't hear what you just said," I say as I place my hand on her shoulder, trying to offer her some comfort.

She looks up at me, and there's a mixture of sadness and awkwardness on her face.

"My period," she whispers. She covers her face with her hands as she cries harder, and it breaks my heart to see her so upset.

Before our parents died, I would've freaked out just thinking about having this conversation with Mia. Fuck, it still freaks me out, but I shove it down.

I pull her into a hug and press a kiss to the top of her head while slowly rubbing her back.

I have no idea how to help. Do I take her to the drug store and let her get what she needs?

"It's okay." *I take a deep breath and push her back. I hook my finger under her chin and nudge it up so she'll look at me.* "We'll figure this out."

"I took care of it. On the way home from school, I stopped at the store," *she says as she starts to calm down a little.*

"It happened at school?" *Shit, that must've sucked.*

She nods. "Rebecca helped me."

She looks so small and sad, so I wrap my arms around her again and hold her, hoping it will make her feel better.

"It made me realize how much I miss Mom," *she whispers against my chest.*

"I miss them too." *It's all I can say.*

"Do you think it will ever get easier?" *she asks as she looks up at me with tear-filled eyes.*

"I don't know," *I answer honestly.*

16

She wraps her arms around my waist and presses her face into my chest.

"I'm so glad I have you, Rhett. I know I don't say it enough, but thank you for taking care of me," she whispers.

I hold her tighter as I whisper, "I'll always take care of you." I tilt my head and catching her eyes, so she'll see I'm serious, I say, "I'll always put your needs before my own. I don't know what our futures hold, but I promise I will be next to you every step of the way."

———

Not a day has gone by where I haven't kept my promise to Mia. She's the only girl who matters to me. I don't get involved in relationships because I can't risk a girl getting between Mia and me. Then there's the fact that most girls are fucking gold diggers.

I might come across as the joker of the group, but I only trust my friends, Mr. Hayes, and Mia. Carter and I have been best friends since our first day of school. People might not see it, but we're a lot alike. With Carter, what you see is what you get, where I hide behind jokes and one-night stands. The only difference

17

between Carter and me is our reason for not getting involved in any kind of serious relationship. Carter doesn't trust anything female. Because of his mother leaving him, he thinks all women are the same.

Having money has taught me, people only see you as a bank account and not a person with feelings. It's been a hard lesson to learn.

It has to be ten times harder for Carter, seeing as he's the wealthy one in the group. We've all reaped the benefits of being his friends, and thankfully he's known us since before our balls dropped. Otherwise, I'm not so sure he would've let us into his life. If it's hard for me to trust people, it has to be next to impossible for Carter.

Jaxson and Marcus have their own reasons for not wanting to commit themselves to a girl. Fuck, Marcus' nightmarish past damaged him for life. He won't let anyone in but Jaxson, and we don't blame him. Carter, Logan, and I understand his reasons for keeping everyone at a safe distance. We might not be as close to him as Jaxson is, but that doesn't mean we don't have his back. Because of his fucked-up past, we do everything in our power to protect Marcus.

I'm close to Logan as well. He's the only stable one between the five of us, and that's the reason I trust him with Mia. The two lovebirds think I don't notice the way they look at each other. I'll never interfere, though. They have to figure shit out for themselves. There isn't another guy on the face of this planet I would want as a partner for my sister.

A while back, Marcus started the Screw Crew list. It was meant as a joke, but since then it's become a competition between us to see who can fuck the most girls. So far, I'm in the lead, not that I'm proud of myself when I look at all the names. Sure, every single girl knows the deal – it's only a once-off fuck. I don't do repeats. But lately, even that's become boring.

I'm more selective now when it comes to choosing a girl. They have to be open to taking risks, like having sex in a place where we can get caught. They have to be wild, which means I stay away from the innocent-looking ones. The last thing I want to do is scar some poor girl for life.

The girl I was with last night was mindblowing. She gave me a taste of something new. It was the first time I had anal sex, and fuck it was hot. It's also the first time I'm considering fucking the same girl twice, but we didn't even exchange names. It was anonymous, dirty, and daring.

It was perfect.

Fucking her on the dance floor only added to the thrill. To others, it might have looked like we were bumping and grinding against each other, just like everyone else, but I was buried deep in her ass.

I'm slowly becoming addicted to living on the edge. It's the only time I know for sure the girl isn't acting. They need the thrill just as much as I do. It's not about how wealthy I am, but how far I'm willing to go.

Basically, on the outside, I might look like a safe bet, but on the inside, I'm a twisted fuck. It's a secret I keep from the guys, and I sure as fuck don't want Mia finding out.

Chapter 3

Evie

Sitting in the back of the van with the other girls, I glance at their faces, wondering how they can laugh and joke while we're on our way to clean another house.

I'm thankful for the job, and I have no problem with cleaning houses. It's the topless part that gets to me, but beggars can't be choosers, and at the end of the day, it's better than being a sex worker.

We all wear the same uniform, which consists of black high heels, a black g-string, and a black jacket that has the words *Double D's Cleaning Services* scribbled across the back in nauseating bright orange. The shoes are a size too big for me, but I took care of that by stuffing toilet paper in the front.

I keep telling myself it's a million times better than having to whore my body out for a warm meal. At least I still have some control. The clients aren't allowed to touch us. Cleaning their homes topless is only for their viewing pleasure.

It's my third day on the job, and as the van comes to a stop in front of a mansion, my stomach plunges to my feet from the weight of my nerves. I'll never get used to this.

It's only until you can find something better, Evie.

I'll get paid on Friday. It won't be much, but it will be enough to see me through until next Friday. Right now, that's all I can focus on, just making it through every day.

I climb out of the van and wait for all the girls to walk ahead of me. Yesterday, I learned that if I let them go in first, the owner is too busy ogling them to notice me. I'm the youngest and more petite than the other girls. I never thought I'd be thankful for my small breasts, but seeing as the others have more to stare at, I don't get gawked at too much.

Reaching the front door, my stomach tightens, and the little food I've managed to get my hands on threatens to come back up as I walk into the house. My eyes dart around, assessing my surroundings.

The interior reeks of money, and I cringe as I imagine the perverted old man who must live here.

22

Walking into the living room, I immediately notice two men. They're sitting in front of a massive flat-screen TV while eating sandwiches. Seeing the food doesn't help and only makes my stomach growl.

One glances back at us, and surprise ripples through me.

Oh shit. They're not old.

They don't look much older than me. The fact that the men are both good looking doesn't do anything to calm my nerves. So far, we've only been called out to homes of elderly men. My heart begins to beat faster when another man comes down the stairs to my right. The second he sees me, he freezes.

A look of confusion washes over his handsome face as he slowly walks closer. When he sees the other five girls, his mouth drops open.

"What's going on?" he asks the other two men in the living room.

The one stops mid-bite. "They're here for Rhett."

"What the fuck?" Someone growls behind me.

I let out a startled shriek and cower closer to Phoebe and the other girls. I keep forgetting their names and only remember Phoebe's because she's in charge of our group.

Cautiously, I glance at the man who just walked in from outside. He's dressed in running gear. He glances at us, and the intimidating look on his face almost makes my heart beat out of my chest.

These guys are all strong and young, and it makes them more of a threat than any of the elderly men whose houses we've been to. Feeling on edge, I wish I could leave.

"Rhett! Get your ass down here," the guy in running gear hollers.

Oh crap. Oh crap. Oh crap.

I've never felt so uncomfortable and out of place in my entire life, and that's saying a lot seeing as I never belonged anywhere.

"Is the cleaning company here?" Someone asks, and then he appears at the top of the stairs.

For a moment, my heart stops, and I even forget to breathe as the most attractive man I've ever seen comes down the stairs.

Phoebe takes a step forward, blocking my view of him. "We're from Double D's Cleaning Services. We're looking for Mr. Rhett Daniels."

"That would be me," Rhett says as he stops at the bottom of the stairs.

I peek around Phoebe's arm and forget that we're not allowed to make eye contact. I shamelessly stare at Rhett. His eyes are the same dark color as his hair, almost black. Everything about him is striking, from his strong jawline to the cocky grin around his full lips.

"You hired a fucking cleaning service?" The other guy growls again, yanking my attention back to him. It's just in time to see him grab the hem of his shirt, using it to wipe the sweat from his face. My eyes drop down, and they widen. Never in my life have I seen abs like that.

Two. Four. Six. Eight.

When my eyes start to follow the V that leads to his shorts, I quickly glance away.

"I thought I'd arrange a little surprise for you all," Rhett replies, his voice full of laughter.

"We'll get started then," Phoebe says as she unties her belt and slips her jacket off.

My eyes dart around as I take a step back, trying to get behind the other girls. All the guys stare at the girls as they start to strip out of their jackets.

"I'm going to Mia's," one of the guys says, and he doesn't waste time darting out the front door.

I let out a relieved sigh, knowing there's one less guy to deal with.

The two in the living room shrug at each other and then continue to finish their meals while watching a football game.

I swallow hard, and reluctantly I begin to untie the belt of my jacket.

"Come on, Carter," Rhett says to the guy with the amazing abs who walks by him to get to the stairs. "You're going to shower now?"

My eyes dart between them as I finish untying the belt. My fingers dig into the silky fabric of the jacket, but instead of taking it off, I wrap it tighter around me.

Carter looks bored as his eyes sweep over us.

"Yeah, there's nothing down here that's worth my time."

Ouch. I should be thankful that none of us pique his interest, but it still stings.

Phoebe nudges me with an elbow and gives me a look of warning before she walks into the living room to start cleaning.

I swallow hard as I look down at my feet.

Think of the money, Evie.

I loosen my grip on the jacket and start to pull it open, and a wave of shame hits as I glimpse the curves of my breasts.

A hand clamps over mine, startling me. Jerking back, an alarmed shriek escapes my lips. Panic floods every inch of me, but before I can try to free my hand from Rhett's, he steps closer to me.

I wish I could say I'm brave, but I'm not. I'm the kind who runs and hides, instead of fights. Right now, all I want to do is run until my body gives up from exhaustion and hunger.

Rhett lifts his other hand towards my body, and I try to yank free so I can get my butt out of this house.

"Shh… it's okay," Rhett whispers as he takes hold of the jacket and covers my right side that was exposed when I pulled back the first time.

I watch with stunned amazement as he ties the belt of my jacket. When he's done covering me, he turns to the other girls.

"The joke's over. You can all go."

My heart is still beating like crazy as I try to calm my breathing from the fright. While the other girls collect their jackets and put them on, I straighten my own out.

Phoebe comes to stand in front of Rhett. "You still have to pay."

"That's no surprise," Rhett says as he takes a few bills from his wallet.

"Thank you for using Double D's Cleaning Services," Phoebe rambles off with the usual fake enthusiasm she's mastered from doing this kind of work for years.

She walks out of the house, and the other girls are quick to follow. I stick close to the last girl, but before I can get out, fingers clamp around the top of my arm, pulling me back.

With horror, I watch the front door slam shut, then Rhett steps between me and my exit, instantly making my heart hammer against my ribs as a fresh wave of panic engulfs me.

Survival instinct starts to kick in, and my eyes dart around, searching for another way to get out.

"How old are you?"

My head snaps up at hearing Rhett's voice, and I swallow hard before I stutter, "E-e-eighteen."

Rhett gives me a doubtful look, which says he doesn't believe me.

"I have to go. The others are waiting for me." I can hear the fear in my own voice, and I hate that I can't sound brave right now.

Rhett's one eyebrow darts up, and he turns to look out the window next to the door.

"Sorry to tell you this, but your friends just drove off," he says as he turns back to me.

"What?" I gasp and dart forward, but instead of getting to the door so I can yank it open, I slam right into Rhett when he moves in front of me to block my way.

His hands fall hard on my shoulders, and my body starts to shake as an all too familiar fear claws its way up my spine.

Why do things like this keep happening to me? I'm just trying to survive, but somehow I always find myself in trouble.

My breaths burst over my lips as I stare up at Rhett, praying he'll let me go.

His eyes soften as he says, "I'm not going to hurt you. You look nothing over sixteen, so you're definitely not my type. I just want to talk to you."

Yeah, right. I've heard that before.

The second I let my guard down, I'll probably be flat on my back, and there's no way I can let that happen.

I yank my shoulders free from his hold and turn to run, but I'm blocked by Carter, who must've just come down the stairs. My eyes dart to the living room, and I watch with an overwhelming sense of dread as the other two men get up from the couch.

Crap. How am I going to get myself out of this mess?

"Let me go," I whisper, the words drenched with terror. I move closer to the wall behind me, trying to put some distance between the men and myself.

Rhett holds his hands up. "We're not going to hurt you."

"Why would she think we'd hurt her?" Carter asks, his eyes darting between Rhett and me.

Glancing at Carter, Rhett looks a little uncomfortable when he admits, "I held her back so she couldn't leave with the others."

"You did what?" Carter snaps, his features instantly tightening with anger.

With them being distracted, I take my chance and dart for the front door. I grab hold of the knob, but an arm wraps around my waist and yanks me back against a solid wall of muscle.

A scream filled with frustration and fear escapes me, and I wildly try to free myself from the tight grip he has on me.

No! Please, don't let this happen.

"What the fuck are you doing?" Carter shouts.

"Dude, you're scaring the living shit out of her," one of the other guys states the obvious.

My eyes dart around wildly, searching for anything I can use as a weapon while I try to pry my body out of Rhett's hold.

I will claw myself out of this house if I have to.

There's no way I'm going down without a fight.

"Look at her," Rhett shouts back. "She's a fucking kid. Would you let her strip if she was Mia?"

When I first saw Carter, I thought he would be the one to take what he wants. Not Rhett. But as I look at Carter, he seems to be the rational one. Taking a chance and hoping I'm not wrong, I plead, "Please. Please let me go."

Carter's eyes snap over my head, and he gives Rhett a look of warning, which chills me to my bones.

"Let her go right now. We can talk about this."

I'm surprised and relieved when Rhett actually lets me go, but then he walks to the front door and leans against it.

My body is tight with fear, and it takes a lot of willpower to not burst out in tears. I'm both angry and scared out of my mind.

"I just want to talk to you," Rhett says, giving me a pleading look.

My eyes keep darting from one man to the other, waiting for one of them to attack me.

"Nothing's going to happen to you," Carter says suddenly.

I give him a wary look. Just because he helped me doesn't mean I trust him.

"Listen to what Rhett has to say, and then I'll take you back to work."

"Talk," I hiss, keeping my guard up.

"How old are you?" Rhett asks again.

My anger starts to win out over the fear, and I glare at him, wishing I was bigger so I could shove him out of my way.

"Eighteen," I grind the word out between my teeth. "I'd show you proof, but my bag is in my locker at work." For the first time since the other girls left without me, I start to worry about losing my job. "I have to go. I can't afford to lose this job."

Rhett gives me an incredulous look, and I'm scared he won't believe me.

"I really need the money. It's the only way I'll get off the street."

I take a step back when anger tightens Rhett's features.

"You live on the fucking street?" he whispers darkly.

Ugh, maybe I shouldn't have mentioned that.

Now Rhett knows no one will come looking for me if he kills me.

Rhett glances at Carter, who shakes his head before Rhett brings his eyes back to me. I don't know what the silent interaction between them means. A fist closes around my heart, and I hold my breath, every muscle in my body tensing for a fight.

"Why aren't you in school instead of cleaning houses topless?" Rhett asks, catching me totally by surprise.

"School?" I squeak. "I'm trying to earn enough for a place to stay, never mind studying." Hoping I'll get out of here, I quickly add, "But if you keep me here any longer, I won't have a job to go back to."

"I'll make you a deal," Rhett says, making my eyes bulge, while my fear increases tenfold.

"I'm not sleeping with you for money," I hiss.

Rhett pulls a face as if the idea of sleeping with me disgusts him. I don't even feel offended at his reaction because I'm too relieved. If he finds me repulsive, then he won't rape me.

"Like I said before, you're not my type."

I wrap my arms around my waist, praying he'll get to the point so I can leave.

"Do you want to go to school?" he asks.

I glance up at the ceiling in frustration. "That doesn't matter." I throw my arms wide and yell, "I'm going to lose my job!"

"If you had another choice, would you go back to school?" Rhett asks again, ignoring my outburst.

"Of course," I snap. "But I don't have a choice."

I suppress the urge to stomp my foot like a ten-year-old or knee him in the junk. With my luck, I'll get arrested for assaulting him.

"I'll pay for your education if you quit this job."

Huh?

My thoughts screech to a halt, and I can only stare at him because he probably lost his mind.

"Yeah, right." I let out a bitter chuckle.

"I'm serious," Rhett says.

I lock eyes with him for the first time, and I get the same twinge in my chest that I got the first time I saw him.

"I'll pay for your education. I'll make sure you have a place to stay as well."

I narrow my eyes at him, waiting to hear what the catch is. If I've learned one thing in life, it's that nothing is for free. There's always a price to pay.

"Why would you do that? You don't know me. What will I have to do in return?"

He looks at me for a few seconds, and then he tilts his head and says, "Just keep your clothes on."

Is this guy for real?

I frown at him. "You'll basically pay me to keep my clothes on?"

"That's right."

My eyes dart to the other men, but they all look as stunned as me.

"I don't get it," I say as I look back to Rhett. "Why would you help me?"

Rhett's eyes sweep over my body in a way that makes me feel like I belong in a dumpster.

If this man dislikes me so much, why in the world would he want to help me?

"You're skinny as fuck. Seriously, you look younger than my sister. You need help, so let me help you. One day you can help someone else again."

I pull a confused face. "You're just going to help me out of the goodness of your heart?" My voice is loaded with sarcasm.

He actually thinks about it before he answers, "Something like that." He locks those intense dark eyes of his on me. "What do you have to lose?"

Chapter 4

Rhett

Every time the door to the registration office opens, I can't help but look. I've been waiting close to an hour, and it's clear the girl's not going to show.

I didn't expect her to come, but a part of me still hoped she would.

The guys all think I'm insane, and I'm starting to agree with them. I don't know what came over me. All I keep thinking is Mia could've been Evie. If Mr. Hayes didn't help us after our parents died, we could've ended up living on the streets.

Evie... fuck, I don't even know her last name. The second I saw her, it felt like the ground opened beneath my feet. She seriously looks like a starving kid. A kid who was about to strip down and clean my fucking house.

A wave of sickening anger slams hard into my gut. What the fuck is wrong with this world that kids live on the street?

I might be a twisted fucker, but I'll never be able to turn a blind eye to a woman or kid who needs help. Dad taught me men are stronger for a reason, and it's to protect women and children.

I get up, not having a fucking clue how I'm going to find Evie. I only know her first name, where she works and that she lives on the fucking street. She wouldn't tell me anything else about herself, not that I blame her. I would've done the same thing if I were in her shoes.

As I walk towards the parking area, I glance across the campus, but there's still no sign of her. When I get to my car, I feel frustrated with the whole situation.

There's no way I can just give up, so I decide to drive to the dump she works at. When I get to Double D's Cleaning Services, I park my car across the street and make myself comfortable. I'll wait here all day if I have to.

I slouch down in the driver's seat and make myself as comfortable as possible. I only manage to wait ten minutes before impatience gets the better of me.

"Fuck this," I growl and getting out of the car, I cross the street. I shove the door open and stalk towards the reception counter.

The receptionist seems bored out of her mind until she spots me. Immediately she sits up, and a smile spreads across her face. Everything about her looks dried out, from her frizzy hair to her face that's covered with makeup.

"I'm looking for Evie," I cut to the chase.

"All the girls are out on calls, but I have a lunch break in twenty minutes," she says, winking at me.

I ignore the bold offer and let my eyes sweep over the sparse furniture.

The pissed-off look on my face quickly makes her smile dry up. "What time will Evie be back?"

"The name doesn't ring a bell," she says, probably being a bitch because I won't give her the time of day.

A man comes out of an office and drops a piece of paper on the reception counter. "Get the sale up on the website," he barks at the receptionist.

I doubt he'll be of any help, but it doesn't stop me from taking a step in his direction. "I'm looking for Evie. She works here."

He turns to me with an irritated look settling on his face. "I fired her ass. I'm not a pimp, so get off my fucking property."

For a second, I'm tempted to punch the sneer off his face, but thankfully I manage to not lose my temper. I don't spare the door from my anger, though, slamming it so hard it makes the glass vibrate.

What the fuck do I do now?

I'll have to search the streets for the kid. I won't stop worrying until I know she's safe.

I pull my phone from my pocket and dial Carter's number.

"You know you missed class, right?" he answers.

"I don't care," I say before I get to the heart of the problem. "Evie was a no-show this morning."

"Who?" he asks, sounding confused.

"That kid from yesterday. Evie," I say, letting out an impatient sigh.

"You're wasting your time, Rhett."

I know he's right, but I can't just give up.

"I'm going to drive around a bit. I have to try to find her."

When he keeps quiet for a couple of seconds, I can picture him shaking his head.

"Come get me. You can't drive and look for her alone."

"Thanks, I owe you."

I cut the call, shove the phone back in my pocket, and rush back to my car. The entire drive home, I keep glancing around, hoping I'll get lucky.

I know Carter thinks I'm insane for wanting to help this girl, and I don't know how to explain it to him, so he'll understand why it's so important to me. Saying I want to do for her what Mr. Hayes did for me, doesn't begin to sum it up. It's a combination of things.

One thing is certain, there's no way Evie's eighteen. Mia looks older than Evie, and she just turned fifteen.

I think what got to me most was how scared and embarrassed she looked. I don't know anything about her past, but there's no way someone like her will make it out on the street.

When I stop in front of the house, I only have to wait a few seconds before Carter comes out. He comes to the driver's side, and I let the window down so I can hear what he wants to say.

"I can't remember what the girl looks like. I'll drive while you search for her."

I shove the door open and walk around the car to the passenger side. I can't believe Carter can't remember her. I'll recognize Evie from her red hair alone, never mind those green eyes. Even though she's skinny as fuck, it doesn't hide her beauty.

Carter starts the car, and asks, "What's it with you and this girl?"

"She's a kid, Carter. I can't let her live on the streets. She won't make it out there."

Carter shakes his head, not agreeing with me.

"I might be helping, but it doesn't mean I agree with you. You can't save people like her. She'll keep going back to the street, no matter how hard you try."

I glare at him before turning my eyes to the window, searching for any sign of her. "Nothing you say will stop me from trying."

Carter lets out a heavy breath, but at least he keeps driving.

"Where do you want to start looking?" he asks.

"I don't know." I think about it for a minute then say, "Close to restaurants and fast food places. If I were homeless, I would stay close to any place where I can get food."

Hours later, I'm on the verge of losing hope when Carter says, "I'm stopping at McDonald's. You want something?"

I have no appetite, which alone says a lot about my mood. I've never been so upset over a stranger before.

"Just get me a bottle of water."

When we pull up to the drive-thru, there are six cars ahead of us.

Without thinking it through, I open the door. "I'm going to look around while you get your food."

I'm out of the car before Carter can respond. Walking through the parking area, I head away from the main street. When I pass by the dumpsters, the stench is almost overwhelming. I carry on down a quieter road, looking up every alley.

I only realize how far I've walked when Carter pulls up next to me. The pissed off glare I get from him tells me he's ready to head home.

I can't give up yet. I know I'll find Evie if I just keep looking.

When I don't get back in the car, Carter gets out and growls, "What the fuck are you doing, Rhett? We've been driving around for hours. Get your ass in the car. We're going home."

"No." I start to walk away from him. "She could be in the next alley."

"Rhett!" he yells at the same time a cry echoes from nearby.

I start to run in the direction I heard the cry come from. It sounded like a woman. If it's a cry for help, I sure as hell won't ignore it.

"Fuck!" Carter shouts, and he slams the car door closed.

I turn up an alley, and except for a couple of dumpsters, it's empty. For a moment, I doubt that I ran in the right direction.

"Rhett, this is fucking crazy," Carter snaps when he catches up to me.

Frustrated that this entire day has been a fucking waste, I shake my head. If I just knew Evie's okay, I'd feel better.

Carter places his hand on my shoulder, and I know he's trying his best to understand my insane decision to find Evie.

"I get you want to help her, but she's gone. For all you know, she's already on her way to another town. You tried, Rhett, but it's time to go home."

"Yeah, you're –" My words are cut off by another cry, and this time it's fucking close. I run towards the dumpsters, and only when I've passed the first two, do I see a flash of red hair.

Hearing a loud bang behind the dumpster, I move around it, and then anger and shock ripple through me.

After being slammed against the dumpster, Evie falls down to the ground, but immediately darts back to her feet. I'm so fucking relieved that I've found her, it makes me freeze for a second.

"This is my alley," a homeless man roars at her.

Darting forward, I step between them. My heartbeat spikes, and my anger quickly turns into rage while I stare the man down.

I fucking dare you, asshole.

Reaching behind me, I take hold of Evie's arm. The last thing I want is for her to run while I face-off with the insane sucker in front of me.

"She's leaving. There's no reason for this to get ugly," I try to reason with the guy.

"This is my alley," he roars again, and from his bloodshot eyes, it's clear he's either on something, or he got his hands on alcohol. Fuck, I don't want to beat up a homeless guy, but I will if he becomes a threat.

"We're leaving," I growl and pushing Evie to the side, I keep my eyes on the guy while Carter takes her from me.

Only when Carter starts to walk away with Evie safely at his side, do I begin to back away.

As soon as there's a safe distance between myself and the homeless guy, he loses interest in me and sits down next to a battered box, which must be his home.

I jog to catch up with Carter and Evie, and I'm surprised she's not fighting us.

What if she got hurt?

I take hold of her arm and pull her to a stop. When I lift her face up, her skin is pale, and her eyes are big from shock.

"Are you hurt?" I ask, glancing over her body, but the baggy clothes she's wearing just about covers every inch of her. She looks skinnier than yesterday. It's like she's vanishing right in front of my eyes.

A wave of protectiveness surges through me, making me want to pick her up and carry her away from this life. Everyone deserves a chance at a good life, and there's nothing I want more than to be that chance for her.

She shakes her head, but her chin starts to quiver. "I didn't know it was his alley," she whispers, and a tear escapes her eye. "I was looking through the dumpsters when he caught me. I tried to explain, but he wouldn't listen."

I glance back to make sure the guy isn't following us, but luckily, there's no sign of him.

I place my arm around her shoulders and draw her to my side. Her whole body's trembling, and it makes me hold her a little tighter. She's so damn small, the top of her head barely reaches my chest.

"It looked like he was on something. Let's get out of here."

She doesn't put up a fight until we reach the car. Pulling away from me, she glances back to make sure she's safe from that guy before she faces us.

The fear in her eyes is a clear indication that she still sees me as a threat.

Before she can start to panic, I say, "I just want to help you. Let me drop you off at a hotel so you'll at least be safe for the night. We can talk about everything tomorrow after you've eaten something and had a good night's rest."

Her green eyes are filled with uncertainty as she wraps her arms around her waist. She looks torn between accepting my offer and running.

I keep my distance from her, not wanting to spook her any more than she already is.

"Evie, if I wanted to hurt you, I would've already. I really just want to help you. We don't have to take my car. We can grab a cab. Let's just get you a room at a hotel so you can be safe for the night. We can meet for breakfast tomorrow and talk about the deal some more. Just give me a chance to help you."

A sad look washes over her face, making her eyes look bruised.

"Okay," she whispers.

Relief rushes through me, making me take a deep breath, then I turn to Carter, who's been watching us silently. "Will you take the car home?"

"Are you going to take a cab home?" he asks.

"Yeah, but I'll call you from the hotel. I just want to get Evie settled."

"Right," he says. He knows me better than anyone else, which means he knows I won't leave that hotel until I've talked to Evie, and I know she's off the street.

At least he doesn't argue. "Catch you later. I watch him get in the car, and as he drives away, Evie and I start to walk towards McDonald's.

"You want to get something to eat while I call for a cab?"

I watch her swallow hard, and then she nods, a look of hunger replacing the sadness that was there a second ago.

I'm taking it as a win. The longer Evie's in my company, seeing that I won't hurt her, the better the odds are that she'll take the deal.

Chapter 5

Evie

Walking into McDonald's, I feel self-conscious. My skin prickles as people glance at me before quickly dropping their eyes again.

It doesn't help that Rhett is right next to me. Even in my desperate state, I notice how attractive he is, and the expensive charcoal shirt and jeans, only make the drabs I'm wearing stand out like a sore thumb. I look like a piece of trash walking next to him.

I ignore the urge to run because I'm way too hungry to lose out on a free meal. The delicious smell hanging in the air makes my stomach growl painfully. A cloud of embarrassment hangs over my head, and I wrap my arms tighter around my stomach, hoping to muffle the loud rumbling.

I'm painfully aware of what I look like until I see the menu with all the pictures of food up on the wall.

"What would you like?" Rhett asks. His deep voice reluctantly makes me tear my eyes away from the menu.

When I hesitate to answer, he leans a little down and whispers, "You can choose anything." When I hesitate, he adds, "Or I'll order half the menu."

My eyes dart back up to the menu, and I feel so overwhelmed by all the choices that I can't make myself choose.

"I'm not picky," I whisper, my cheeks flaming up with shame.

A month ago, I would've died just thinking about being in a situation like this, but after living on the streets the past weeks, my need to survive far out weights my battered pride.

When it's our turn to order, and Rhett steps up to the counter, I can't force my legs to follow. I stand rooted to the spot, my cheeks burn hotter. I'm so caught up in this mortifying moment that I jerk when Rhett takes hold of my arm. I let him pull me out of the line, to the side where we have to wait for the order.

I'm thankful when Rhett takes his phone out and starts to type on it, instead of trying to have a conversation with me.

When the order is ready, Rhett hands me the cups. "Will you grab us some soda while I get us a table?"

I nod, and keeping my head down, I make my way over to the soda fountain. I blindly go with the first option and fill the cups.

When I turn around, I'm relieved to see that Rhett chose a table in the back. Feeling vulnerable, I quickly walk to where he is. I place the cups in the middle of the table and sit down as fast as I can. Hunching my shoulders, I let my hair fall over my face so I can hide behind it.

Rhett moves a tray into my line of vision, and the moment I see the burger, chicken nuggets, and fries, tears push up my throat. With trembling hands, I pick up a nugget. At first, I try to hold myself back as I take a tiny bite, but when the rich flavor explodes in my mouth, I lose all my self-control. I shove the entire nugget in my mouth and savor the taste and warmth as tears spill from my eyes.

I quickly wipe them away and self-consciously glance at Rhett, hoping he's not witnessing the lowest moment of my life.

His eyes are locked on my face, his features torn with anger and anguish, and it only makes more tears rush to the surface.

"I'm sorry," I whisper.

I try harder to stay in control of my emotions and hunger while I reach for the second nugget, but my hand freezes an inch away from the golden-brown piece of chicken when Rhett growls, "You have nothing to apologize for."

I wipe my cheeks again, and feeling uneasy and ashamed, I dart another glance at Rhett. I wish I could take the food and go hide somewhere private so I can savor every bite.

"Don't worry about me or the other people, Evie. Please eat."

I try to blink the tears away, and with a slight nod, I pick up another nugget.

I've just swallowed my third nugget when Rhett pushes one of the cups closer to me. I give him a trembling smile as I bring the cup to my lips. Taking a tiny sip, a sickly sweetness engulfs my mouth, and I immediately regret not getting water for myself.

"I've ordered us an Uber. It should be here in ten minutes."

Yesterday, I had a job and the strength to fight, but after being fired and spending another night on the streets, I'm desperate.

Maybe Rhett really wants to help me?

It's not like I have many options. I'm either going to die on the streets or take a chance and hope for the best.

I'm torn up between feeling hopeful and scared out of my mind, as I stare down at my full tray of food. I can only manage one more nugget before I'm full, and I stare at the burger and fries with a sense of loss.

"If you've had enough, you can take the leftovers with you."

Rhett only has to tell me once. I close the lid over the box and carefully place it in a paper bag Rhett must've asked for when he got the order. When the little packet of fries is also inside the bag, I carefully close the bag so I won't tear it.

"Are you ready?" Rhett asks.

When I nod, he gets up and taking our trays he disposes of them before I follow him outside to where a car's already waiting for us.

He holds open the door for me, and for a second, I hesitate before I climb into the back seat. When Rhett gets in next to me, my hand instinctively moves closer to the handle of the door next to me, so I can quickly escape if I need to.

Rhett gives the driver the name of a hotel, and as the Uber takes us to the destination, I remain painfully aware of Rhett sitting next to me.

Holding the bag of food tightly, I take in my surroundings when we're dropped off in front of a hotel, that's way too luxurious for the likes of me.

Rhett pays the driver, and once we're out of the car, he lightly takes hold of my elbow.

There's a war raging inside of me as we walk toward the entrance, and entering an expensive but stunning reception area, I'm once again reminded that I look like something the cat dragged in.

Every surface sparkles and even the plants by the fountain look like they've been polished. To my left, I notice a boutique filled with elegant clothes. To my right are plush couches, and a man who's seated at one frowns at me from over the top of his newspaper.

I hold my bag of food tighter, and unconsciously I take a step closer to Rhett while we walk to the reception counter.

"I'd like a room for one person," he says as he takes his wallet from his back pocket.

I don't make eye contact with the pretty brunette behind the counter. The last thing I want to see is the gleam of disgust in her eyes when she looks at me.

"Only for one person?" she asks, and I hear the disapproval clearly in her tone.

Oh no, she thinks I'm spending the night with Rhett.

"The lady will be staying alone," he bites the words out.

When I glance up at him, I'm surprised to see the look of warning he's giving the receptionist.

I've never had someone stand up for me. To some people, it might be nothing, but the fact that Rhett just defended me, leaves me speechless.

Rhett's behavior keeps catching me off guard because after he's done checking me into the hotel, he hands me the keycard to the room. I stare at the little card, not quite believing that I'll have a safe place to stay for the night. I feel a flutter of excitement in my chest, but I warn myself to not let my guard down. Life has a way of hitting me off my feet the moment I think things might be getting better.

"You're on the second floor, room two-o-four. Make sure you lock the door behind you. I'll meet you right here tomorrow morning at nine. We can have breakfast, and then you can tell me whether you're taking the deal. Please think about it tonight. There are no strings attached. I really just want to help you."

"You're not coming up?" I ask, surprised.

He frowns down at me.

Oh crap! I didn't mean it like that.

"I... that came out wrong. I just thought you would like to talk now. It's not like you know me, and you're about to leave me alone in an expensive-looking hotel. Aren't you scared that I'll steal something?"

Ugh, that sounds even worse.

I close my eyes, and my face starts to light up with embarrassment.

When I feel his hand on my shoulder, my eyes snap open. He gives me a light squeeze before removing his hand.

"I thought you would feel safer if I didn't go to the room with you. If you want to talk now, I'm all for it. Honestly, it would make me feel better."

I nod as I force a small smile on my face.

"I'm not going to lie, it will be awkward, but the sooner we talk, the sooner we'll feel comfortable around each other. We might as well talk now, it's not like I have any plans for tonight."

"Okay, let's do this," he says.

The silence is uncomfortable as we get in the elevator, and it keeps getting thicker while we walk to the room. I have zero social skills and don't know how to approach this situation.

When we get to the door, I'm not sure what to do, so I hold the keycard out to Rhett.

He takes it from me, and I don't miss as the corner of his mouth twitches. He swipes the card and pushes the door open. When he waits for me to walk in first, I feel a warmth blossoming in my chest.

My eyes dart around the room, and my mouth falls open from seeing all the luxury.

"Wow," I whisper, totally awe-struck by how stunning the room is. There's even a tiny lounge with plush couches and a TV. I can't remember when last I watched TV.

"Do you like it?" Rhett asks.

I glance over my shoulder to where he's still standing in the doorway.

"It's beautiful," I say. Placing my bag next to the couch, I smile at Rhett. "You can come inside."

He walks a little closer, his eyes quickly sweeping over the room.

We're back to being awkward, and wanting to break the ice, I ask, "Why are you doing this for me? You don't know me."

A soft look fills his eyes, and it feels like he's giving me a glimpse of himself. Looking at him now, he doesn't come across as someone who would hurt me. Yesterday I was scared out of my mind, but after he's done nothing but help me the past few hours. I'm starting to think that I might have overreacted a little.

"A man once gave my sister and me a chance. He kept us from living on the streets, and I want to give you the same chance."

"Thank you," I whisper. I wonder if Rhett understands what this means to someone like me. "I don't know what made you look at me yesterday, but I'm so thankful you did. All of this," I sweep my hand over the room, "is so much more than I could ask for. But the fact that you saw me when everyone else kept looking right through me, I have no words to describe what that means to me."

The look on his face is gentle. "You're welcome, Evie."

He moves slowly towards me as if he's worried that I'll run off if he walks too fast.

This day started out horrible, and if someone told me I would end my day in a luxury hotel, and allow a man I've just met to hug me, I would've thought they were crazy.

But here I am, and I don't stop Rhett as his arms wrap around me. Resting my cheek against his chest, I pinch my eyes closed.

How is it possible such a kindhearted and remarkable person like Rhett sees someone as ordinary as me?

Just being noticed by another human being fills me with the profound thought that I'm not invisible. For a moment, it feels like I matter. It's food for my battered soul, and in a way, I needed it more than I needed shelter and nourishment.

When he pulls back, his smile is kind. The gentle look in his eyes only makes me feel more at ease.

Rhett holds the keycard out to me, and when I take it from him, he says, "I'm going to leave so you can get some rest. I'll be back early tomorrow morning. We can talk then."

He walks to the door, and as he starts to shut it behind him, I take a step forward. "Rhett!"

The door instantly swings open, and a worried look tightens his features.

"In case something happens, I just want you to know that you've already made a difference in my life."

"Nothing's going to happen, Evie. I'll see you tomorrow."

I nod and stand still as he closes the door behind him. It sounded like a promise, but nothing is set in stone.

At least for tonight, I'll be safe, warm, and fed.

Chapter 6

Rhett

As I get into the elevator, I send Carter a message, letting him know that I'll be home soon. Shoving the phone back in my pocket, I wait for the doors to open, and then walk to the reception counter.

The receptionist gives me a knowing look. She must've seen me get in the elevator with Evie. I don't care about her assumptions as I scowl at her.

"Can you have dinner sent up to room two-o-four?" I ask when she looks at me with a fake smile.

"I can place the order with our restaurant. What would you like?"

I give her points for remaining professional.

"Anything healthy," I say, not sure what Evie would prefer. I should've asked her what she wanted to eat before I left. "Send up a platter with a variety of foods."

"What time should we send it up?"

Evie will probably want to bathe first, and she still has the burger and fries. I glance at my watch and notice that it's almost six o'clock.

"Can you send it up at seven?"

"I'll have a platter sent up at seven. Will there be anything else?"

"No, I guess that's everything," I say. There's no reason for me to stick around any longer. Before I leave, I ask, "Can you call me if Evie checks out before I'm back?"

This time the receptionist frowns. "You're not staying?"

I glare at her, not liking that she's nosy. People need to learn to keep their fucking noses out of other people's business.

"No. I'm not. Call me if she leaves," I growl, and not waiting for her to agree, I turn around and stalk toward the exit.

Just before I reach the doors, I notice the clothing store to my right. Not sure if Evie has anything clean to wear, I make a quick decision to get something for her.

Walking into the store, a lady approaches me with a smile. "Can I help you, sir?"

"Yeah, I have a friend staying here for the night. I don't know her size, though. Could you send someone up to her room to get her size and then send her ..." I glance at the clothing, not sure what Evie would like.

"I can help put an outfit together if you tell me what your friend's plans are for tomorrow," she offers.

She's probably going to run.

The thought doesn't sit well in my gut.

"We're going apartment hunting."

"Something comfortable then. Should we charge it to your bill?"

"Please." I follow the lady to a counter where she grabs a piece of paper and a pen. Realizing she needs Evie's information, I quickly give the details before thanking the lady.

Once outside, I call myself an Uber. I don't like leaving her here, but I'm in desperate need of a shower and sleep after the long day.

Getting home, I'm not surprised when I walk into the living room, only to find all the guys waiting for me.

"Evie's staying at a hotel tonight. Hopefully, she'll be there tomorrow morning."

They all keep quiet and continue to just stare at me, which prompts me to say, "I'm going to help her get on her feet. That's all."

Still, they say nothing, which starts to annoy me.

"Stop looking at me like that," I growl.

Logan gets up and shakes his head. "Can you blame us? You've never shown interest in committing to a woman before. We're all a little shocked."

"I'm not committing to a woman," I quickly defend myself. "I'm helping a kid. There's a huge difference."

Logan chuckles as Carter gets up and walks over to me. When he's standing in front of me, he says, "Evie's not a kid, Rhett. She's eighteen. Whether you like it or not, taking care of her means you're going to have to be committed to her in some way. This isn't something you can start and stop at the drop of a hat. Make sure you're in it for the long run."

Fuck, he's right.

Jaxson surprises me when he says, "This isn't a pet project, dude. This is a person's life. This girl is going to be dependent on you, so you better not fuck with her. It's your choice to help her, and that comes with some major responsibility."

"I know," I grind the words out. Not wanting to hear another warning, I turn around and head for the stairs.

I take a shower, the entire time thinking about Evie. No matter how pissed I got at the guys for voicing the obvious, I have to face the facts. Evie will be my responsibility.

As terrifying as the thought is, I can't turn my back on her. Watching her eat earlier, tore a hole in my heart. I've never seen anything so heartbreaking. Fuck, don't even get me started on when she thanked me for seeing her. It gutted me. How fucking alone must a person be if they feel the need to thank someone for noticing them? I can't comprehend it.

I might have dealt with some shit in my life, but I can't remember a single day where I've felt alone. I've always had someone.

I told Evie I'm going to help her, and it's a promise I will keep.

Chapter 7

Evie

Still, feeling overwhelmed, I stare at the clothes I've laid out on the massive bed. I can't believe Rhett did this for me.

I was sitting on the couch, thinking about everything Rhett had already done for me when the woman knocked on the door. I thought it was Rhett, but after opening, the woman from the boutique explained she was here to take my measurements.

The cream cashmere sweater is the softest thing I've ever felt. I lightly trace the tips of my fingers over the fabric as a smile forms on my lips.

All the luxury is a lot to take in. Growing up, I never had anything I could call my own. I still don't, but for tonight, I'm going to pretend this is all mine. I might never get a chance like this again.

I walk to the extravagant bathroom and fill the tub with steaming water. I can't wait to soak in it. Brushing my fingers over the towels, I notice a collection of bath products on the counter. Lifting a tiny bottle of shampoo, I unscrew the cap and take a deep breath of it. It smells divine, like a bouquet of flowers.

Another knock at the door has me quickly screwing the cap back on. I place the bottle back with the others and rush to the door.

"Who is it?" I ask while peeking through the peephole.

"Room service." I can see part of someone dressed in white, and a cart with silver dinnerware on it.

When I open the door, an elderly man pushes the cart into the room and turns to me. "Where can I place it for you?"

I point to the living room, wondering if he didn't make a mistake.

"I didn't order anything," I say.

"The order was placed with reception. Enjoy your dinner," he says before leaving the room.

I close the door and walk over to the cart. When I lift one of the lids, and I see a spread of fresh fruit, my mouth instantly begins to water.

I'll never be able to repay Rhett for all his kindness.

I take the plate of fruit to the bathroom and strip out of my dirty clothes while shoving grapes into my mouth. When I sink down into the hot water, I let out a happy sigh. I let the warmth seep into my bones while I eat most of the fruit. With a satisfied stomach, I lie back and close my eyes.

When the water turns cool, I add hot water before washing my hair. Being able to use beauty products fills me with excitement, and I can't help but laugh out loud as contentment fills my chest.

When I'm clean from head to toe, I dry myself with one of the fluffy towels. Taking a complimentary robe from behind the door, I put it on.

There's even a toothbrush and paste, which I don't hesitate to use. This room has everything I could ever need, and by the time I've dried my hair, I feel more like a woman and less like trash.

Careful not to wrinkle the new clothes, I hang them in the closet, then crawl into bed and let out a bliss-filled sigh as I snuggle into the plush pillow.

"Thank you, Rhett," I whisper as I snuggle deeper under the covers.

I can't remember if I've ever slept as well as I did last night. I've taken another bath before getting dressed in the new clothes Rhett got for me.

I've been staring at my reflection for so long that I've lost track of time. I'm clean, and the beautiful sweater, jeans, and boots make me feel feminine. It's something I haven't felt before.

I even have new lace underwear on.

My hair frames my face with light curls, which brings out the green of my eyes. I might be way too skinny, but after all the pampering, I feel pretty.

I make the bed and clean the bathroom before I wash my clothes in the bath. After I've thanked Rhett, I'll find a spot where I can let them dry in the sun, so for now, I place them in one of the plastic laundry bags I found in the closet.

I feel guilty when I place the tiny bottles of beauty products in my bag, and I hope I won't get caught with them. I stuff as much of the food as I can into the paper bag I got at McDonald's, and when everything I own is packed in my bag, I glance around the room one more time.

Feeling a little sad, I remind myself to be grateful for the experience. I take a deep breath before I leave the room, and with my energy replenished, I walk to the elevators.

When I walk out into the reception area, there's no sign of Rhett, and for the first time, I think he might not come to meet me this morning.

Hoping he will show up, I take a seat on one of the couches and watch the entrance.

As time goes by, I start to grow anxious. I glance down at the keycard in my hand as my thoughts turn to the deal Rhett offered me.

I want to jump at the chance, but my pride keeps me from saying yes.

I can always pay him back.

I frown at the thought. I haven't considered it before. If I take the deal, I'll be able to study and get a good job. I can pay Rhett back once I start working. It could be a loan.

My heartbeat speeds up with hope as I consider all the possibilities.

But... can I trust Rhett?

The thought puts a damper on my excitement until I remind myself Rhett could've hurt me already if that was his plan. He has been nothing but kind to me.

I glance up at the entrance, still undecided about what I should do, and when Rhett walks in, my heart skips a beat. A tremor of nerves sets in as my eyes follow him.

I've been so caught up in my troubles that I haven't really looked at Rhett again since I saw him coming down the stairs at his house. Now that I'm feeling rested and I'm not so scared, I take a few seconds to examine him.

He's wearing blue jeans and a white t-shirt today. I notice the tattoo that covers his entire left arm all the way to his knuckles. Even though he's dressed casually, he still looks like a force to be dealt with. Every movement he makes exudes confidence, which only adds to his already incredible good looks.

Not taking my eyes off Rhett, I get up and nervously clutch my hands together in front of me.

His dark eyes skim over me as he scans the area. A worried look crosses his features before he glances in my direction again. This time he doesn't look away as he slows to a stop in the middle of the reception area.

I start to feel self-aware and painfully anxious as he continues to just stare at me. When it borders on awkward, he finally moves, stalking toward me.

I swallow hard and force a smile to my face when he stops right in front of me. He opens his mouth, but no words come out, so I take my chance. "Thank you, Rhett. I really appreciate what you've done for me." I'm happy when I don't fumble over the words.

A slow smile begins to form around his mouth, which makes my heart do a cartwheel. At least it doesn't look like he regrets helping me. That would've sucked.

"Morning, Evie, you look great. I forgot to ask last night, but can I see your I.D.?"

Caught off guard, a nervous feeling slithers down my spine. I unzip the front of my bag and remove the card. Handing it to him, I wait anxiously while he inspects it.

With a stunned look, he says, "Damn, you really are eighteen."

He hands it back to me, and I quickly tuck it back in the front pocket so I won't lose it.

When I glance up at Rhett again, there's a sexy grin on his face, which makes my stomach flutter, and I quickly look down at the floor. I can't think of Rhett as sexy or attractive.

Yep, that's asking for trouble I don't need.

"Are you ready for breakfast?" he asks.

Still unsure about taking his deal, I hope having breakfast with him will help me decide.

Chapter 8

Rhett

Fuck, I can't believe what one night of sleeping in a decent bed, having a bath, and getting some food in her body has done for Evie's appearance. I almost didn't recognize her.

Evie Cole. I got her last name from her I.D. card. I would never have believed she's eighteen if I didn't see it with my own eyes.

She's only a year and five months younger than me. Hopeful that I'll get to know her better, I choose a table at the back of the room, so we'll have privacy.

I pull her chair out, and the blush creeping over her face tells me she's not used to this kind of treatment. It's actually refreshing being around Evie. The women I usually go out with take everything for granted.

After I've taken the seat across from her, we study the menu.

"Morning, I'm Beth, and I'll be your waitress," a perky blonde says with a wide smile. It's a nice change from the receptionist.

"I'll just have coffee," I say, not hungry at all.

Evie orders the same, and as soon as the waitress is out of hearing distance, I say, "You can order breakfast."

"I've never been a big eater early in the morning. Coffee is good."

She fidgets with the keycard, and I reach across the table to take it from her. My hand almost covers both of hers as I give her an encouraging squeeze before pulling back.

"Let's get to know each other a little. I think it will help calm your nerves."

"Okay," she whispers, but her eyes don't meet mine, which tells me it's going to take a lot to get her to feel at ease around me.

"You know my name. Rhett Daniels. I'm nineteen. What else?" I try to think of something else to say that won't be too personal.

"The other men you live with, are they your brothers?"

Happy that she asked something, I smile as I answer, "We might not be related by blood, but they are my brothers. Carter and I have been friends since our first day of school."

"Carter seems nice," she says, and I don't miss that she's not as tense as when we sat down.

"Actually, Logan is the nice one. I think you're the first person to describe Carter as nice." I might have meant it as a joke, but there's a lot of truth to it. Carter is realistic and doesn't take shit from anyone.

There's a moment of uncomfortable silence between us. I'm not used to awkward moments with girls. Usually, there isn't any time for awkward moments because I never have conversations with any of the women I sleep with.

But Evie is different. If she's going to be my responsibility, then we'll have to get comfortable with each other.

"Do you have any brothers or sisters?" I ask, just as the waitress brings our coffee.

While I wait for her to answer, I add cream and sugar to my cup.

"No," she whispers before she takes a sip of her coffee.

"Do you have any family?" After placing the cup down, I cross my arms on the table, giving Evie my full attention.

"No."

She doesn't elaborate, which only makes me wonder more about the life she's had.

"What happened to your parents?"

She shrugs, and finally, she looks up from her hands. Meeting my gaze, I don't like the lost look I see on her face and wish I could change her past.

Just when I think that she's not going to answer me, she says, "I don't know. I've never had parents."

I frown, unable to believe she doesn't know her own parents.

"I've been in foster care since I can remember," she explains.

Shit, at least Mia and I have good memories of our parents.

"How did you end up living on the street?"

She drops her eyes back to her hands, and I know I've just hit a sensitive subject.

"I turned eighteen." Again she doesn't elaborate, and I decide to drop that subject for now.

"Don't take offense, but I have to ask. Have you ever been arrested?"

She cringes and whispers, "No, and before you ask, I haven't done drugs either."

"That's good to know." I take a sip of my coffee before I continue. "Have you thought about the deal?"

"I have." Her eyes meet mine, and I see the uncertainty, which gives me hope that I can still convince her. "Can you explain it to me again?"

"It's quite simple. I'll be your benefactor, and in return, all you do is study your ass off. The only rule I have is that you keep your clothes on. No stripping. No dating. Give your full attention to your studies."

"What rights will you have as my benefactor?"

I immediately read between the lines. "Evie, I'm going to be straightforward with you. I have no hidden agenda."

She bites her bottom lip, still worried about my intentions.

"Hey," I whisper as I reach across the table and cover her hand with mine, hoping that I'm not too forward by touching her. "I want to give you a chance to be independent."

She lets out a soft sound through her nose, almost like a silent laugh. "I still don't understand why you're willing to help me. Especially when you aren't getting anything in return."

"I have a sister. She's a few years younger than you. Living on the streets could've been our fate if Carter's dad didn't take us in when our parents died. He didn't have to, and he certainly got nothing in return. Like I said yesterday, I want to give you the same chance I was given."

"It's all surreal," she whispers as she pulls her hand from mine. "If I take the deal, what will I have to study?"

I smile, knowing she's going to agree.

"You can choose. We will look at apartments together, and the lease will be in my name, but you will have a say in which apartment we go with. I'm not sure what to do about your monthly expenses. I'm not comfortable with just transferring funds to your bank account."

"I don't have a bank account," she says, her cheeks flushing pink.

"We'll figure something out. I'll pay the school fees and rent. Maybe we can go together once every two weeks to get anything you might need, and that way, I can also check in with you to see how your studies are going?"

"We could do that." She realizes what she just said when I grin at her.

"That sounded like a yes," I tease her. She smiles, and it transforms her face. "You need to smile more, Evie."

Emotion washes over her face, and her voice is hoarse when she says, "You've given me a reason to smile. I don't know how to thank you."

"Become a beautiful, independent woman. That will be thank you enough for me."

"I don't know about the beautiful part, but I really want to be independent," she replies, a smile tugging at her mouth again.

I reach over the table and wait for her to shake my hand. When she does, I say, "We have a deal, Evie Cole."

"It's a deal," she says, and a burst of laughter is quickly smothered by a sob. "I'm sorry."

I give her a moment to compose herself. It's understandable that she's emotional right now.

Once she's in control of her emotions, I say, "Let's go apartment hunting."

"Right now?" she asks, her eyes sparkling with excitement. It's another look which suits her.

"Right now." I get up. "Are you okay with staying here until you can move into an apartment?"

Evie hesitates before she answers, "This place is expensive, Rhett. I'll be fine at a motel."

Just because she keeps trying to get out of me spending money on her, it makes me want to give her everything her heart desires.

"I'll feel better if you stay here," I say, hoping to change her mind about the motel.

"Okay," she whispers with the bright smile back on her face. "But hopefully, it won't be for too long, and we can find a reasonably priced apartment."

Chapter 9

Evie

I hope this isn't all a dream.

I catch myself smiling as Rhett drives to another apartment. I've been laughing so much today that my cheeks ache. It's wonderful. We've already seen three places that were way too big and expensive.

At the last one, we argued for the first time. Accepting Rhett's help doesn't mean I'll let him get an apartment that's bigger than any house I've ever lived in. That's just crazy.

When he stops outside another luxurious building, I scowl.

"I can already tell you I'm not going to agree," I say as he opens his door.

"You haven't even seen it yet," he says, grinning at me.

"Can't we look in a normal neighborhood where the rent will be reasonable?" I ask, but he gets out of the car before I've even finished my sentence.

When I open my door, he says, "Let's just have a look."

I relent and follow him to the second floor. When we walk inside, I'm actually relieved to see the kitchen is much smaller than the other ones we've seen.

The living room is also a decent size, and I love all the light streaming in through the large windows.

I turn in a full circle and frown when I count three bedrooms. That's a bummer.

"I only need one bedroom," I say.

"You can use one of the other bedrooms for a study," Rhett starts to argue.

"I don't need an extra room for a study. One bedroom will be fine. I can also study in the living room."

"Woman, will you stop being stubborn for one second. This apartment is situated in a nice area. My house is right around the corner." He actually rolls his eyes at me. "You know most women would just say thank you and take it."

I frown at him, not missing that it's the first time since we've met that he's called me a *woman* and not a kid. *And twice in a row.*

I get a feeling Rhett is used to giving money out as if it were smiles. If that's the case, he's got another thing coming.

"All this space is a waste of money, Rhett."

"You can always rent out the other two rooms." He walks closer to me, trying to stare me into submission, which almost works. One look from those dark eyes is enough to make me lose my ability to think, never mind form a coherent sentence.

"I don't know anyone," I mumble, feeling lame that I'm admitting something like that to him.

Rhett takes a deep breath, then pins me with a penetrating look. I'm not sure I like the look. It makes me feel self-conscious around him. It's as if he's trying to figure out what I'm thinking.

I won't even try to deny that Rhett's way too much male for me to handle. Knowing he isn't much older than me, and adding that he's been nothing but kind to me, only makes him so much more attractive. There are moments where I feel at ease with him, but then there are instances like this one where I feel way out of my comfort zone.

When we were viewing the second apartment, Rhett took hold of my hand to hold me back when I wanted to leave, and it made my stomach flutter, and I've been cautious ever since.

I have to be careful that I don't mistake feeling grateful for attraction. Besides, Rhett's made it clear I'm not his type, so it would be a waste of time on my part anyway.

"You'll meet girls once you start classes. I'm sure you'll make friends."

I take a step back and breaking eye contact with him, I glance around the apartment again.

"I'm sure everyone attending school will already have a place to stay."

"I'm going to put in an application."

"That doesn't mean I'll move in here," I throw at him over my shoulder.

"Dammit, Evie. It's a safe neighborhood. You're close to the school. I live right around the corner. This place is perfect."

Turning to face him, I cross my arms and glare at him. "It's too much."

"Too much what? Money? Last time I checked, that was my problem," he snaps as he starts to lose his patience with me.

"You don't like hearing the word no, do you?" I ask, realizing Rhett is used to getting his way. "I know it's your money, Rhett. Trust me, I'm highly aware of that fact." Once the words are out, I pinch my eyes shut. I didn't mean for it to sound so harsh. I let out a sigh and drop my arms to my side. "I'm sorry, that was uncalled for. I'm grateful for all your help. Not only is this place costly, but it's too much for me. I've never had my own bedroom before. I wouldn't know what to do with all this space. I'd rather have something small and comfy than something big and empty."

I give Rhett a pleading look, hoping he'll read between the lines. All this space will only remind me that I'm alone.

"I really like this place." My hope goes up in a puff of smoke. Rhett's too stubborn to see things from my point of view. "Just try it for three months. If you can't find roommates, then we can look at smaller places."

My eyes dart back to his. "Really? You'll be okay with that?"

"Yeah," he says, smiling. "Can I go fill in the application now?"

"It's not like anything I say will stop you from doing what you want," I tease.

"You're a quick learner, Evie Cole," he jokes back. "Stick with me, and I'll make you famous."

Laughter bubbles over my lips. It amazes me that the one second we can be arguing and the next we're laughing. I've never met anyone like Rhett. Being around him is actually pleasant, and it makes it easy to like him. I think it's the same for him because he's starting to joke with me.

Six months later.

As I pull the brush through my hair, I stare at my reflection in the mirror.

Everything has changed over the last few months. It happened so fast that I'm still overwhelmed when I think about it.

Living on my own has been an adjustment. Before I met Rhett, I had to worry about surviving, where now I have too much time, and it makes me feel lonely.

I'm still looking for a job, but at least now, I'm able to be more selective in my choices. I'm hoping to hear back from the gas station down the road. Yesterday I applied for the cashier position, and with a little luck, I'll get it.

During the first three months, I used to see Rhett a lot, but since I've started studying, I only see him once a month. He had me open a bank account, so he could easily transfer money into it, instead of having to go shopping with me. He gives me way too much, but I only use what I need. The rest I leave, hoping once I'm done studying, I'll be able to repay him much quicker.

If I'm honest with myself, I have to admit I miss Rhett. He crawled into my heart those first two weeks. I thought we were becoming friends, but seeing as he chose to put distance between us, I must've been mistaken.

I stand up and take one last look at myself before I grab the sweater from where it's lying on the bed, along with my bag. Since I've gained back all the weight I lost while living on the streets, I've been experimenting with clothes. I scour all the thrift stores for bargains, and that way, I'm able to save a good portion of the monthly allowance I receive from Rhett.

It's getting colder, but with the boots and sweater, I should be fine wearing a dress today. I fell in love with the dress the second I saw it. It's vintage with a high waist and a pleated skirt. The bodice is cream, which complements the deep green skirt.

Walking out of the apartment, I have to admit I actually feel pretty. It's a foreign feeling, but one I bask in.

I haven't decided what to study yet, but luckily I have plenty of time before I have to decide on a major.

I get to class with some time to spare, and doodle in the front of my notebook, when a girl sits down next to me. I smile at her before returning to my not so great drawing of a palm tree.

"Damn, I should've grabbed a coffee. I was worried I would be late for class if I stopped to get some," the girl sitting beside me says.

I drop my pen on the table and smiling at her, I say, "Coffee would be nice." Glancing at the time, I see that there are only five minutes until class starts. "I don't think we could get some and be back in five minutes."

"Yeah, this lecture is going to be torture without my caffeine fix. I'm Willow," she says.

"I'm Evie."

We share a smile, and I just know I'm going to like her. She's tall and beautiful. Her blonde hair looks silky soft, and intelligence shines in her warm, brown eyes.

"I love your hair," I can't help but pay her a compliment.

She lets out a burst of laughter. "It takes me thirty minutes to straighten it like this. I usually just leave it to air dry, but then it curls like crazy."

I point to my curly mop of red hair. "Nothing can straighten this mess."

We have to pay attention when the professor comes in, but I can't stop smiling. It's nice talking to a girl.

When class is over, I shove all my stuff into my bag.

"Do you have another class now?" Willow asks.

"No, I only have one later this afternoon," I say. Right now, I want to get something to eat and a cup of coffee.

"Want to join me for coffee?"

"That would be great." I should've thought to ask her. Maybe we can get to know each other and become friends.

The cafeteria is bustling with students, all looking for a caffeine fix after class. We grab our orders, and I choose a muffin for myself while Willow takes a bagel. We pick a table outside, for which I'm grateful. It's freezing in the cafeteria.

With the sun baking on my back, I enjoy some of my coffee before I ask, "Do you live on campus?"

Willow rolls her eyes and lets out a sigh. "I do. My roommate drives me insane, though. She's out every night, and when she comes in late, she makes one hell of a noise."

A slow smile spreads across my face. I feel a little embarrassed and nervous as I say, "I have an apartment off-campus, and I'm looking for roommates. You're welcome to come to look at it."

Willow's eyes widen with surprise. "I'd love to see your apartment. It would be wonderful to sleep an entire night through without being woken up."

"We can go now. I don't have any plans," I offer.

"Are you sure?" she asks, excitement coloring her cheeks a pale pink.

"Trust me, I'm desperate for a roommate. The silence in the big place is killing me."

"Do you want me to follow you?"

I frown, and for a minute, I don't understand what she's asking.

"My car is parked in front of my dorm. If I'm going to follow you, I need to go get it quickly," she explains.

"Oh no, don't worry about that. The apartment is close by. We can walk if you don't mind."

We finish our coffee and breakfast before we walk to the apartment. All the way there, I'm silently sending up prayers that Willow will like it enough to want to move in with me.

Chapter 10

Rhett

I duck behind a tree when I spot Evie coming out of the cafeteria. I'm a dick for avoiding her.

It's just... I'm fucked.

When she started gaining a healthy amount of weight, her appearance changed. It was like watching a butterfly slowly open its wings.

Yeah, she's healthy now, and I'm happy for her, but it's not so great when it comes to my dick. Her breasts filled out and damn... that ass of hers. It went from as flat as a surfboard to plump and firm. Her skin now has a healthy glow, and her hair shines, which makes the strands look like flames.

Basically, every time I see her, my dick forgets she's off-limits, and it goes rock hard. The little shit doesn't understand the meaning of *friends only*. She's definitely not someone I can screw around with. She's been through enough shit as it is. The last thing she needs is me hooking up with her for a random fuck. With her being dependent on me, it's made it hard to be around her. *Pun intended.*

The first time I got hard, she was bending over to tie a shoelace. I was so shocked by my physical reaction to her that I high-tailed it out of there at the speed of light. I haven't been back to her apartment since. I always meet her in a public place, and I stick to once a month. It's safer that way.

That's why I'm hiding behind a tree like a five-year-old. Until I've figured out a way to get my dick to calm down, I can't be around her.

I wait for Evie to walk past the tree before I head towards the cafeteria. I need to do something about this problem. I can't keep avoiding her.

Fuck, it's not that I even want Evie. Not in a sexual way. She's not my type. But my dick seems to have a mind of its own whenever she's around.

I've had a few one-night stands, but it's done nothing to satisfy me. I need something more, something wild.

Yeah, that will take my mind off Evie's ass.

Once inside, I glance around for a suitable candidate. I might as well start looking now. With a little luck, I can get laid before my next class.

"Well, well, well, if it isn't Rhett Daniels. What do us mere mortals owe this honor to?" I look down at Josie as she runs a finger down my arm.

Damn, I'm not that desperate.

Or am I?

Fuck, this chick has been trying to get into my pants since the start of school.

"What's up?" I ask to buy myself some time to make up my mind.

To screw Josie or not to screw Josie, now that's one hell of a question.

She brushes her hand down my chest until it comes to rest on my belt buckle.

"We could go somewhere, and I could show you what's up," she says, trying to come across as sexy but failing miserably. It sounds like her sinuses are clogged up.

My eyes drop to her chest. Her breasts are a little too big for my taste. Then again, if I fuck her from behind, I won't have to look at her face.

Deciding to test the water to see just how desperate Josie is to get into my pants, I lean closer to her. "You've been trying for a while now. What will you do for me to screw you?"

Her lips part as she sucks in a breath, and her lashes lower. Instead of it being a turn on, she looks like she's about to fall asleep.

Fuck, I can't read this chick's facial expressions to save my life. Is she horny or sleepy?

"I'll do anything you want me to."

Horny, it is then.

I glance around, thinking of a place we can go. A random fuck in the back seat of my car isn't going to cut it. I need something exciting, a place where there's a chance that we might get caught. I need that adrenaline to make me forget about Evie's totally fuckable ass.

"Let's go," I say as I start to walk in the direction of the library.

Josie keeps up with my long strides, and I know I'm an asshole for not walking slower, but I couldn't give a flying fuck right now.

As I enter the library, the old, musty smell of books slams into my face. Yeah, I try to avoid coming here.

Most of the students are downstairs, so I take the stairs up to where the reference books are. I think I've only been up here twice, and it was against my will.

I keep going past the rows of shelves until I reach the back. When I turn to face Josie, my shoulders slump. This girl seriously doesn't do it for me. I have no desire to see her naked.

When she drops to her knees, and her fingers work on loosening my belt, I feel a wave of relief wash over me.

She pulls down the zip and works to free my cock from my boxers. It's a good thing I'm a shower and not a grower, or Josie would be holding a flaccid, shriveled dick right now.

As she leans in to take me in her mouth, I let my head fall back and close my eyes. She's surprisingly good at giving head, and not slobbering or biting me like some other girls do.

I bring up the image of the girl I fucked in the club a couple of months back, and it sends tingles racing down my spine. Remembering how I took her from behind, makes a groan build up in my throat.

I open my eyes and scanning the aisle we're in, I picture what it would be like if someone walked in on us. Excitement bubbles in my chest, and it's just what I need.

My hips start to thrust forward as pleasure builds in my abdomen. I close my eyes, fully intent on fantasizing about the girl from the club, but instead, a clear image of Evie's ass and tits fill my mind.

The image is so vivid that I instantly blow my load, not giving Josie any warning. Thankfully, she doesn't have a problem swallowing.

As she wipes her mouth with the back of her hand, I slip my dick back into my pants and fasten my belt.

She stands up, looking proud of the fact that she got me off so fast. Not wanting to hurt her feelings, I give her shoulder a squeeze.

"Thanks, babe."

I walk away, knowing it's a dick move, but it's not like I promised her anything in return.

As I get to the stairs, my stomach sinks at the sight of Evie coming up.

Just my fucking luck.

She's wearing a loose-fitting dress with black stockings and boots, and I have to say she looks absolutely beautiful. She has her hair up in a bun, but a few tendrils have escaped. I've never seen her hair up before. It gives me an unobstructed view of her face and those fuck-me-senseless green eyes.

There's a soft smile playing on her lips, but when our eyes meet, it begins to fade. She slows down and looks uncomfortable when she reaches the top.

"Hey," she says, her eyes doing a wild dance around the room, instead of looking at me. Then she frowns as her eyes land on something behind me.

An arm curls through mine, and I close my eyes for a second. Shit, I forgot about Josie.

Before I can drag Josie away from Evie, Josie narrows her eyes and sneers, "Oh wow, someone apparently missed the memo about the sixties being over a few decades ago." The flash of hurt on Evie's face makes me move to take a step forward, but Josie holds me back. She presses a kiss to my cheek and loudly purrs, "Thanks for letting me suck your cock. Maybe we can go somewhere more private next time, and I'll show you what I can do with my hips."

Pins and needles spread out over every inch of my skin.

What the fuck?

I can't believe Josie just said that.

Evie sucks in a sharp breath. This time the look on her face makes me want to shove Josie down the stairs so I can take Evie in my arms. I hate seeing the hurt in her eyes.

Before I can try to explain my way out of this shit storm, Evie swings around and rushes down the stairs.

"You're such a bitch. I knew I kept dodging you for a reason." I growl at Josie as I yank my arm free.

"Yeah, but now that I've had my lips around your cock, you'll be coming back for more," she says, smiling as if I didn't just insult her.

"In your fucking dreams. I'm not into crazy chicks," I snap before I turn my back on her, effectively dismissing Josie. I take the stairs two at a time, so I can catch up to Evie.

I have no fucking clue how I'm going to make this right. First, I avoid Evie, then she practically catches me with my pants around my knees while a bitch deep throats me.

This day couldn't get any worse.

Chapter 11

Evie

As I push through the wide glass doors of the library and step outside, thunder rumbles overhead.

Just my luck. The sky is dark, and as drops start to fall, I walk quickly towards the pavement. Hopefully, it doesn't begin to pour before I can get home.

The thought isn't even cold when there's another crack of thunder, and it starts to rain heavily. The drops are big and fat, soaking my clothes within seconds.

Being wet in the cold makes my body start to tremble. For a crazy second, I contemplate running back to the library so I can take shelter until the storm passes, but then I remember Rhett and the girl he was with.

I'm not even sure why seeing him with a girl hurts so much. It's not like I'm friends with Rhett. Hell, I'm nothing but a charity case.

Just thinking that makes me feel grateful once more that I got the job at the gas station. When they called me this morning, I was so surprised. I've been unsuccessful with so many other applications that I didn't think I would get the position. Even though I'll be working nights, I'm excited that I finally got a decent job, especially one where they don't require me to remove my clothes.

But still, there's an ache in my chest when I think of what Rhett and that girl were busy doing seconds before I got there.

A blowjob at the library! Never mind that it happened in a public place, I never thought of Rhett as a man with needs. For some reason, knowing this about him has changed how I always saw him. I used to see him as some savior of sorts, but now... now I'm forced to see the man. I worked hard to ignore the initial attraction I felt towards him. Not that I'm suddenly feeling attracted to him. It's just that... ugh, I don't know what it is.

"You're silly, Evie!" I mutter under my breath. "It's not like you see him a lot anyway."

The thunder rolls again, and I can swear I hear my name.

When lightning strikes nearby, I let out a startled shriek. Someone grabs hold of my arm, it gives me such a fright that I immediately yank my arm free. The sudden movement makes me lose my balance. Unable to catch myself, I fall, and my butt slams into the pavement with such a force, I feel the vibration all the way to my teeth.

"Fuck." The harsh growl above me has my eyes darting up.

The sight of Rhett towering over me makes me swallow hard. His shirt is soaked through, making the fabric stick to his broad chest and showing off every sculpted muscle. Drops of water run down his face, and his dark eyes and hair make him look like a fierce god.

Well, no need to keep sitting at his feet. It's not like his savior complex needs a boost.

When he reaches a hand out to help me up, I ignore it and climb to my feet. I adjust the strap of my book bag over my shoulder and take a step back.

"I didn't mean to scare you. I called, but you didn't hear me," Rhett explains.

"It's fine." I point to behind me. "I have to go. It's raining."

Way to go, Evie. Like the man doesn't know that it's pouring.

"Let me give you a ride home. You can't walk in this weather," Rhett says as I start to turn around.

I'm shaking my head before he's even done talking. There's no way I can be alone in a car with him right now. I'm too embarrassed from knowing about the blowjob. The ride home will only be painfully awkward.

"I like walking in the rain," I say, but my shivering from the cold doesn't make me sound very convincing.

Time to make a run for it, Evie.

"See you around." The words rush from me as I spin on my heel, walking away as quickly as I can without falling down again.

The next second, strong fingers take hold of my arm, and I'm whirled back around. I slam into Rhett, and before I can recover from the shock, he bends down, presses his shoulder against my stomach, and then I'm airborne.

"What are you doing?" I shriek as my book bag tumbles to the ground. I'm too busy clinging to the soaked fabric on his back to try to stop my bag from landing on the pavement.

"It's wet and fucking cold out here, woman," Rhett growls as he plucks my bag from the ground.

I try to wiggle my body out of his grip, but his arm tightens over the back of my thighs.

"Rhett!" I hiss through my teeth, dumbfounded by his caveman behavior. "Put me down."

I place my hands flat on his back and feeling his hard muscles flexing beneath my palms, almost makes me forget that he has me upside down over his shoulder. I shake my head lightly to rid my traitorous mind of the foolish trance a few muscles has it ensnared in, and start to wiggle again.

A wet slap to my bottom makes my eyes widen, and my lips part as a tiny peep rushes from me.

Rhett just slapped me on the butt.

"You can't walk home in this weather," he says, calmly, as if this isn't... crap, I don't even have words for what this situation is. Nothing like this has happened to me before.

When I hear whistles and Rhett's name being cheered from a nearby dorm, I pinch my eyes shut. My cheeks start to flame with embarrassment from other students witnessing this absolutely crazy moment.

I'm so thrown by what just happened that I remain speechless until we reach his car.

I hear my bag falling to the ground with a wet slap. Rhett moves his hands to my hips and pulls me down the front of his body, and it makes my breath whoosh from me as my feet meet the ground. It doesn't help at all that my dress has bunched up between us, and my thighs are exposed to the whole world.

I yank my hands back from where I was gripping his shoulders, but the tight grip he has on my hips keeps me from putting a safe distance between us.

My eyes dart up to his, and I should let him have a piece of my mind for tossing me over his shoulder, but my mouth dries up the instant our gazes meet. His eyes are so dark and intense that my stomach flutters with something I'd rather not name.

"Yo," my mind snaps derisively, *"don't even think about going there. Get me out of the gutter."*

I open my mouth, but still, nothing comes out. I must look like a gaping fish right now.

"He's off-limits, silly girl," my mind adds her two cents as if I wasn't aware of that glaring fact that keeps slapping me upside the head whenever I have a moment of weakness, and I dare think that Rhett is hot... and

dark… and broody… and sexy … and damn, I'm so screwed.

His eyes finally release mine, but then they travel down my body and gets stuck on my thighs, which has me quickly reaching down between us, so I can try to straighten the wet fabric out.

It feels as if his heated gaze is scorching every inch of my icy skin, which isn't helping at all.

"It's no use," my mind sighs sullenly. *"You're definitely screwed. When this blows up in your face, don't come crying that I didn't warn you."*

His fingers tighten their grip on my hips, only making me more aware of him as a man. It also makes me realize why I'm upset about what that girl said in the library.

I want Rhett to notice me. Not as the homeless girl, he needs to take care of, but as a woman.

The thought is so jarring and unexpected that I rip my body free from his hold. I grab my bag and walk around the car to the passenger side.

Breathlessly I say, "Fine. If you want your car wet, it's your loss. Can we leave already? I need to get home."

I yank the door open and climbing into the car, I swear I hear him muttering under his breath, "It's not the only thing I want wet."

Chapter 12

Rhett

Fuuuuck!

Yeah, that's about the only reason I have for my behavior. Oh, right, that's not an explanation at all.

Dickhead.

Asshole.

Dipshit.

What the hell am I doing?

I climb into the car and try as I might, my eyes go straight to her breasts, and it doesn't help that it's only covered with a thin layer of wet nothing. It might as well be nothing. I have a perfect view of her tits. The flawless swells. And don't even get me started on those nipples.

Biteable, suckable, lickable nipples.

The stuff wet dreams are made of.

I shift in the seat, trying to move into a more comfortable position, so it doesn't feel like my zipper is trying to strangle my rock-hard cock.

As I pull away, Evie finally catches her bearings and scowls at me. "Why did you throw me over your shoulder?"

Because I couldn't bear the sight of your perfect tits a second longer without fucking you right there on the pavement.

Because I didn't want any of the other guys on campus seeing your hot as fuck body in a wet dress.

Because... fuck, there are a million reasons.

Of course, I don't admit that. Instead, I clear my throat and growl, "In case you haven't noticed, it's raining, and we're both soaked."

Anything is better than telling her the truth. I'm pretty sure the last thing she wants to hear is that I have a new image to fantasize about when I rub one out in the shower.

Fuck, this is insane. I hardly know Evie. Well, besides her basic info, but nothing about who she is, what she likes, what makes her tick.

What makes her tick. Now there's a subject I'm interested in.

It's official. I'm a fucking pervert. I swear my brain's default setting is sex, sex, and... oh yeah, anything to do with sex. Add images of Evie wearing a wet dress, and you have a winning recipe for a mind-blowing orgasm.

I let out a heavy sigh as I try to focus on the road.

"That's no reason for throwing me over your shoulder," Evie mumbles, refusing to let go of the trivial matter of me acting like a dick. "You could've just asked me to get in the car."

My eyebrow darts up, and I give her a skeptical look. "Babe, I'm pretty sure I did ask you." I nod my head, pretending to think about what happened. "Yeah, right before your stubborn ass said you're fine to walk home in the freezing storm."

She narrows her eyes, and finally, she has mercy on my poor dick as she crosses her arms over those mouthwatering tits of hers.

I pull up to my house, and when I stop, Evie says, "Uhm, Rhett. This is your place."

I frown as I look at her. "Your point being?"

She widens her eyes at me as if she's questioning my sanity. Actually, she should question my sanity.

Hell, I'm pretty sure I would rank high on the crazy-as-fuck-meter.

"I don't live here," she snaps incredulously. "You know what," she adds as she opens the door. "Don't worry. I'll walk from here."

Before she can even get around the car, I'm out of my seat and stalking towards her. I'm fucking cold, wet, and horny. I'm definitely not in the mood to run after her.

I grab her, and without a second thought, I throw her over my shoulder again. Her shriek brings a smile to my face, but her hands digging into my back only makes me harder.

Ignoring the grumbling coming from behind me, I walk towards the front door. When Evie starts to squirm, I let out a soft chuckle then plant my hand firmly on her ass. She lets out a startled squeak while her entire body freezes.

Once inside the house, I head up the stairs, and I only stop when I'm in my room. I kick the door shut behind us before I lower her to the floor, and just because I like to torture myself, I let her body slowly brush against mine on the way down, which makes her dress bundle above her thighs.

Yeah, I'm definitely a sucker for punishment.

Instead of staying plastered to me like she did earlier, Evie steps away while glaring daggers my way. "Why do you keep doing that?" She quickly pushes the fabric down her legs.

I shrug as I pull the wet shirt from my body, and when I start to undo my belt, Evie's eyes widen, and she shrieks, "What are you doing?"

"Ahh… I'm getting out of the wet clothes because I'm fucking cold. I thought it was pretty obvious," I shoot at her as I shove the drenched jeans down my legs.

Evie's mouth opens and closes a couple of times while her eyes zero in on my chest before they skip down to my abs, and land on my cock, which is thankfully not at full mast due to the cold.

That's until my eyes land on her tits, and thanks to the rain we just walked through, the top part of her dress is practically see-through.

"Go shower," I growl at her as I turn away so she won't see my rapidly hardening cock.

"Shower?" she gulps behind me.

I drag on a pair of sweats and grab the first shirt I see and throw it at Evie. Needing some distance from her so I can get rid of the hard-on, I snap, "Go shower. The last thing I need right now is for you to get sick."

I immediately regret my harsh words when she looks at me as if I just drove over her puppy, then backed up to go over it again.

"Evie," I whisper full of regret, but she shakes her head and rushes into the bathroom.

When I hear her lock the door behind her, I close my eyes as remorse and anger pool in my chest until it feels like I might choke on it.

I brought Evie here so I could apologize for what happened at the library. It wasn't to insult her while drooling over her like a boy who just discovered that girls have the magical power to make his dick hard while turning his brain into nothing but a flaccid muscle that's of no use.

"Get your shit together!" I whisper angrily, annoyed with the unexplained strong physical reaction I have towards Evie.

I grab one of Mia's sweatpants that somehow ended up in my closet again and go knock on the bathroom door.

"I have sweats you can wear." When Evie doesn't unlock the door and remains silent, I place it on the floor. "I'll leave it at the door. I'm going to make some coffee. Take your time in there."

"Thank you." The words are soft, but I can still hear how dismayed she sounds, and it guts me that I'm the reason for it.

"Hey, look," I say, feeling like an idiot for talking to a closed door, "I'm sorry for being an asshole. I tend to act first and think later."

"It's okay."

This time her voice is a little louder, but it does nothing to make me feel better about being a world-class dick.

Chapter 13

Evie

I'm standing with my back resting against the door as Rhett apologizes.

Only when the cold becomes unbearable, and I'm shivering uncontrollably, do I open the door slightly. I'm relieved to see that Rhett is not in the room, and I quickly pick up the sweats. I close and lock the door before I let the water run so it can warm up first.

Stripping off my clothes isn't easy as it sticks to my skin like glue. When I'm finally undressed, steam fills the bathroom. I step into the shower and lean my forehead against the tiles as the warm water chases the chill from my body.

My mind turns to everything that's happened today. For five months, Rhett has basically ignored me, and now this? I don't understand any of it or his weird behavior.

The man even stripped down to his boxers in front of me.

My face flushes as I remember every muscle and inch of golden skin my eyes got to feast on. I've never had a crush on a guy before. Hell, I was too busy surviving to think about the opposite sex, or dating for that matter. But whenever I see Rhett, my hormones sit up and notice while my heart swoons.

I know nothing can ever come of it, but it sure doesn't stop me from hoping.

I should be angry with Rhett for tossing me over his shoulder like that, and for bringing me here instead of taking me home, but I can't.

A smile plays around my mouth because I liked it a little too much when he turned all caveman on me.

And the two slaps to my butt?

My stomach flutters and my skin tingles just from remembering what it felt like to have his hands on my body, even if it wasn't meant to be sexual.

Sigh, I reach for the soap and start to wash my body when I remember how harsh he spoke to me. All the good feelings evaporate into the steam, and my heart grows heavy.

The only reason I didn't argue with him about showering here is that he said the last thing he needs is me getting sick. He thinks it will cost him more money should I ever get ill, but he's wrong. Now that I have a job of my own, I'm going to start taking care of myself. Soon I'll be able to tell Rhett he doesn't need to pay for anything else, and I'll be in a position where I can begin to repay him everything I owe.

When I'm done showering, and my body is warm, I quickly dry myself off before stepping into the sweats. They're a bit too big, and I have to roll the waistband over a few times. Pulling on the shirt, it falls to my butt, and I pull a face at the unflattering sight.

Picking up my wet clothes, I hope I can use Rhett's dryer, that way I won't have to stay in this oversized outfit for too long.

I feel out of place as I go in search of Rhett.

I haven't seen any of Rhett's friends since he started helping me, and I'm hoping that I don't run into any of them.

Walking through the living room, I hope I'm heading in the right direction.

When I get to the kitchen, I see Rhett where he's drinking coffee while staring out the window. He's still shirtless, and the view of his muscled back sends tingles racing through my body. Even though he was rude to me, I can't be angry with him.

My eyes drop to his butt, and I let out a breathy sigh. He's got one hell of a sexy behind. I should know. I had a close-up view of it earlier.

He turns around, and my eyes dart up to his face, hoping he didn't catch me gawking at him.

"Come get some coffee," he says.

I take a few steps forward before I remember the wet clothes in my hands.

"Do you have a dryer I can use?"

He sets down his cup, and the movement draws my gaze to his chest. I wish he would put on a shirt because it's way too distracting to have him running around without one on.

"Yeah, sure."

I follow him into the laundry room that's twice the size of my kitchen. I wonder if the guys even do their own laundry.

Shoving my clothes into the dryer, I set the timer. When I'm done, I wipe my hands on the sides of my pants and turn to face Rhett. He's standing much closer to me than I expected, and I take a step backward, only to bump into the dryer.

Feeling out of sorts, I tuck some wet strands behind my ear before pointing to the kitchen.

"Coffee... ahh... I'll make some." Ugh, I'm an idiot for getting all flustered just because there's a half-naked man in front of me.

I squeeze by him, and when my arm brushes against his, it sends electric jolts darting from my arm to between my legs. It's nothing compared to what I felt when he placed his hand on my butt, but it's enough to jumble my emotions.

I've known Rhett for six months, and I still don't have a clue how to act around him. Whenever he's close by, it feels as if I'm standing on a piece of wood that's being tossed around by waves. Everything becomes wobbly, especially my emotions.

When I see that his cup is empty, I glance at him.

"Can I pour you another cup?"

He comes to stand right by me and leans against the counter with his hip. Crossing his arms over his chest, he says in a rough voice, "Yeah, thanks."

I devour his bulging biceps before I have to tear my eyes away. I'm grateful that I have something to keep my hands busy, even if it's just for a couple of seconds.

I slide his cup closer to him, then take a sip of my own while keeping my eyes glued to the counter in front of me.

"How's school?" he asks.

Yay for a safe topic. I'm used to Rhett asking me questions about school.

"It's good."

I want to ask him how his classes are, but I'm scared he'll think I'm referring to his blowjob session with Josie. Instead, I drink my coffee.

"Tell me about yourself," he says, which makes me swallow hard on the mouthful of coffee.

"Myself?" I say, my voice sounding croaky from the sip that almost ended up in the wrong hole.

"Yeah." Hearing the smile in the one word, I glance at him.

The sexy grin pulling at the corner of his mouth has me clearing my throat before I answer, "But you know everything about me."

"No, I don't," he argues. "Has North Carolina always been home?"

I nod and use the cup as a buffer to hide behind, but too quickly, it's finished. I rinse the cup before walking to the laundry room. I don't care if the clothes are wet. I'll only have to wear them until I get home.

"It takes more than ten minutes for clothes to dry," Rhett says.

"I know," I mutter, feeling a little irritated that he pointed it out. "I have to get home."

Before I can reach the dryer, an arm slips around my waist. Rhett's chest presses against my back as he lifts me off my feet.

Instinctively I grab hold of his forearms. "Put me down."

Rhett chuckles as he walks through the kitchen, never letting go. Only when we reach the living room, does he set me down in front of the couch.

"Sit. We can watch a movie while your clothes dry."

I scowl at him as I plop down on the couch. "Yes, Sir," I say wryly. He's so damn controlling.

When heat flares in his eyes, I regret being so snippy. I quickly look away as I scoot into the corner and bring my legs up to my chest, wrapping my arms around them.

Rhett sits down next to me and teasingly says, "Only women tied to my bed call me sir."

My mouth drops open as my eyes dart to him. I can't believe he just said that.

Chapter 14

Rhett

I put on the first movie I saw.

I realize it's not my brightest move when *IT* pulls Georgie into the drain, and Evie's arms flail out to the sides as she jumps with fright. She accidentally slaps me across the chest before she scrambles over the back of the couch and falls behind it with a thud.

I start to chuckle as I pause the movie. When Evie peeks over the back, I burst out into full-blown laughter. It's the cutest thing I've ever seen.

"Turn it off," she whispers as if *IT* is nearby, and he'll hear if she speaks any louder.

"It's just a movie," I tease, not able to resist taking advantage of the situation.

Her eyes dart to the TV screen and widen with fear when she sees that it's frozen on *IT's* face. All you can see are the clown's teeth.

She ducks back behind the couch, and when I look behind it, it's only to see her crawling towards the stairs.

"What are you doing?" I laugh because this shit is funny as fuck.

"I'm getting away from that thing!" she snaps angrily.

I'm about to tease her some more when the baggy shirt she's wearing drags along the floor, giving me a full view of her swaying tits.

Fuuuck!

I hear the back door slamming shut as one of the guys must've just gotten home, and I shoot up from the couch to get to Evie. I don't want any of the guys getting an eye full of Evie's tits.

I grab her around the waist and pull her up. She screams bloody murder, and it makes Carter come running into the living room, just as I manage to pull the shirt over her stomach with my free hand.

"What the fuck are you doing to her?" Carter roars as his eyes dart between Evie and me.

"Nothing," I say innocently. "We were watching *IT*, and Evie got scared."

Evie wiggles in my arms, trying to get free, but I turn around and head towards the stairs. Her back is still firmly pressed against my chest, and my arm that's wrapped around her waist is caught beneath the shirt, which means I'm skin on skin with her.

Soft skin.

Not thinking, I brush my thumb over her rib. Her hand slaps over mine, stopping me from moving, and she whispers, "Put me down."

Reluctantly, I let go of her, and when she turns around, I'm fascinated by the blush, coloring her cheeks.

"I'm sure the clothes are dry," she mumbles under her breath, but as she tries to dart around me, I take a step to the right, blocking her way.

I should let her go, but I can't. Usually, I have self-control made of steel, but when it comes to Evie, it turns to Jell-O.

"It's already past nine, you might as well stay."

What the fuck did I just say?

Why would I say that?

Oh right, because I'm a sucker for punishment, is why.

127

"I can't stay." She breathes the words incredulously as if it's the most absurd thing she's ever heard.

Maybe she's right, but it seems I'm all for being absurd and not caring a single fuck about how torturous it would be if she stayed over.

Just to prove that I love being in a state of constant arousal, to the point where it's actually painful, I say, "Yes, you can, and you're going to. It's still storming outside. You already showered."

"I can't," she says again, which only makes me more determined to win this argument.

"Give me one good reason why you can't stay," I challenge her.

She peeks to where Carter is sitting in the living room, already watching the business news.

When her eyes come back to me, the blush deepens on her cheeks, and it does something funny in the region of my heart.

"Because, Rhett," she whispers so Carter won't hear. "We don't even know each other that well."

"Woman, I'm asking you to stay over, not to fuck me."

Yeah, I could've been more discreet. The problem is that I want to fuck her, and that's making me act a little crazier than usual.

"You don't have to be so crude!" she snaps. "Why would I want to stay over when it's clear we can't be in each other's company for ten minutes without arguing?"

She has a valid point, but there's no way in hell I'm admitting that to her.

I let out a frustrated sigh. "Look, it's about time we get to know each other a little better, don't you think?"

Her eyebrows are drawn together as she stubbornly stares at me. Then her shoulders slump, and she huffs, "You're not going to give up, are you?"

"Nope." I pop the *P* and grin cockily. "I always get my way." I wag my eyebrows just to taunt her.

She scrunches her nose and rolls her eyes at me. "You don't have to be so cocky about it," she says as she crosses her arms over her chest.

The word cocky from her lips has a direct link to a particular hardening part of my body.

"Say that again," I whisper, smirking as I step closer to her.

A frazzled look crosses her features, and her eyes dart over me as she tries to figure out what I'm up to.

"Say what again?"

"Cocky," I grin.

"Cocky? Why?" She genuinely looks baffled now.

"You never curse," I say. It's something I noticed when we first met. "The dirtiest word you've ever said is cocky."

She lets out a heavy sigh. "Small things amuse small minds," she grumbles.

I take another step closer until we're standing chest to chest, and it surprises me when Evie doesn't move away from me.

"Babe, there's nothing small about me," I growl.

Her eyes widen, and for a moment, they drop to my mouth. I see the spark of heat before she lowers her lashes to hide from me.

Deciding to have some mercy on her, I take hold of her arm just above the elbow.

"Come on, we're just going to talk and sleep. Scouts honor." I pull her lightly, and she gives in, climbing up the stairs with me.

"I doubt you were in the scouts," she says.

Chapter 15

Evie

My mind is screaming for me to go home, but my stubborn heart doesn't want to hear about being sensible right now.

Ugh, I'm going to regret this in the morning.

With every step I take closer to his room, my mind yells, *"What the hell are you doing?"*

"Just chill. We're only going to talk," my heart answers while doing silly cartwheels and sprinkling glitter everywhere.

"Yeah, right, I've heard that one before," my mind says dryly.

Rhett stops at a room and pushes the door open.

"I didn't know you guys were home," he says to someone, and as I peek inside the room, I see a pretty girl with long black hair sitting on a bed next to one of Rhett's friends. They both seem to be typing away on their laptops.

"Yeah, we got home about an hour ago," the guy says as he looks up from his laptop.

"Evie, this is Logan, and the pretty one pretending to do homework is my sister, Mia," Rhett introduces us.

I can see the resemblance between Mia and Rhett, but where Rhett is tall, Mia looks much smaller.

"Nice to meet you both," I say, trying my best to look friendly.

"You brought a girl home?" Mia says as she climbs off the bed. She stops in front of me, and I have to look up to meet her eyes. "I love your hair," she compliments me with a genuine smile.

Self-consciously my hand shoots to the mess on my head. I forgot about it, but it must look awful after I let it air dry.

Mia reaches out and takes hold of my hand so she can pull it away. "I mean it. You have beautiful hair."

A warm smile spreads across my face. "Thank you."

I'm tempted to compliment her back, but I don't want it to sound like it's forced just because she praised me.

Mia lets go of my hand and lifts an eyebrow as she looks at Rhett.

"Don't start with me, squirt," Rhett growls, although his voice is warm with love for his sister.

Mia wags her eyebrows, silently teasing her big brother. It's nice seeing this side of Rhett.

"Evie is just a friend. Get used to seeing her around." Rhett leans closer to Mia and brushes his finger over the tip of her nose. "Now stop being nosy and finish your homework."

She smiles warmly at Rhett before she goes back to the bed.

As we walk away, Rhett leans into me and whispers, "They have the hots for each other, but they think no one knows."

"Oh," I whisper as I glance over my shoulder. "How old is Mia?" I ask, wanting to know more about her.

"She's fifteen."

He doesn't say anything else, so I gently probe, "And you're okay with her dating Logan?"

Rhett shrugs. "Logan would rather die than hurt Mia. I know my sister is safe with him."

Before I can ask another question, a guy comes barreling out of a room, slamming into my side. I lose my balance and fall against Rhett, and when his arms circle me, I become highly aware of the fact that he's still shirtless. My right-hand grabs hold of his lower back, and my left flattens over his chest. My entire front is plastered against his side until he pulls me closer, bringing us chest to chest.

His manly scent and the heat from his body overwhelm me. My heartbeat speeds up as every part of my body, touching his begins to buzz with tiny electric bolts.

"Shit, sorry," the guy says. "You're so small I didn't see you."

"Evie, this is Jaxson. He and Logan are twins," Rhett says, sounding way calmer than I feel. Apparently, he's not affected by our close proximity like I am.

"Hi, Jaxson," I say, trying to not let my rampant emotions seep through to my voice. I'd die if Rhett ever found out how affected I am by him.

"Hey, Evie."

Another guy comes out of the same room Jaxson was just in, and for a second, I can only stare. He is easily the most gorgeous man I've ever laid eyes on. Where Jaxson is blonde like Logan, the new guy is all dark and broody. If someone had told me he and Rhett were brothers, I would've believed them.

"And that's Marcus. His bark is worse than his bite," Rhett says playfully.

What does he mean by Marcus' bark is worse than his bite?

"What-the-fuck-ever," Marcus growls. He gives me a cold look before he shoves past us.

I instinctively inch closer to Rhett, until I feel his chest against my cheek.

A slow grin spreads over Jaxson's face as he says, "You kids have fun now."

Suddenly we're alone in the hallway with Rhett's arms still around me, and it has me quickly pulling back to put a safe distance between us.

Clearing my throat, I say, "Interesting friends you have."

"They're my family. For the last ten years, it's just been us guys, Mia, and Mr. Hayes."

"Mr. Hayes?" I ask, glad that we're back to talking about Rhett's life as we walk to his room.

"Carter's dad. He took us all in and has been taking care of us."

"Oh," I whisper, wondering how they all landed up together. I don't ask, scared it will give Rhett the idea of asking me questions in turn.

When we walk into his room, I glance around, not sure where I should sit.

Rhett plops down on the bed, crossing his arms behind his head.

"Make yourself comfortable, Evie," he says.

All I can do is stare at his lean, hard body, stretched out before me like a feast waiting to be devoured.

I shake my head lightly to rid myself of the stupid fantasies and carefully sit on the edge of the bed by Rhett's feet.

He rolls his eyes at me, then darting forward, he grabs my arm and pulls me back onto the bed with him.

I end up lying stretched out, half on the covers and half over Rhett. My face flames up as I quickly move away, and turning on my side, I stare at the bed until it feels like my face has cooled down a little.

"You're weird," Rhett says, making my eyes snap up to his.

The words sting, and he must see it on my face, because he quickly adds, "Not a bad weird. You're shy, but at the same time, you have all this fight inside of you. It's a weird mixture. I've never met a shy girl who could argue as much as you do."

I'm not sure if it's a compliment or insult, so I decide to keep quiet.

"What are you scared of?" he asks.

I frown at him, not sure what he means.

"I'm scared of…" his words trail away. I sit up and fold my legs under me. "Rats. Fuck, I hate those critters with their beady red eyes."

I start to laugh at the expression on his face. It looks like he stepped in something nasty.

"Well, you know I'm scared of clowns," I say.

He lets out a deep chuckle that does crazy things to my hormones.

"Yeah, I figured as much after you crawled away from me."

"I never watch horror movies," I admit. I don't add that my life has had enough horror. "I like comedies."

"I'll remember that next time we watch a movie." He smiles tenderly at me, and it warms the spot in my chest where my heart is.

Chapter 16

Rhett

I drink in Evie's relaxed smile before my eyes drop to her exposed shoulder, where the shirt has slid down. There's something about this girl that excites and scares me at the same time.

My gut is telling me to stay far away from her, but I can't. Like the gravitational pull of the moon causes waves, she causes those same tides inside of me.

"Which movies do you like?" she asks me, drawing me out of my thoughts.

"Anything really," I whisper, not wanting to disrupt the relaxed atmosphere between us. "If it's entertaining, I'll watch it."

"You know," she says softly, dropping her eyes to her hands, "you're also weird."

I smirk, not surprised. "How so?"

"You come across as this easy-going guy, but then there are moments like this afternoon where you become a neanderthal." She bites her bottom lip as if she's nervous about continuing, but then she pushes through. "I think there are so many sides to you that you don't allow people to see."

She peeks up from under her lashes, and our eyes lock for a moment.

When things become too intense, I chuckle, "Nah, I'm your regular joker, babe."

She shakes her head lightly, a gentle smile, making her look breathtakingly delicate.

"I think it's a wall you use to hide behind."

Her honesty stuns me for a second before I regain my composure.

"Don't we all have our walls?" I ask.

She shrugs, looking back to her hands.

I lean forward and placing my finger under her chin, I nudge her face up. Her eyes find mine as I ask, "What do you hide behind your walls?"

I'm playing a dangerous game right now, and it's going to backfire on me. I drop my hand from Evie's face and let it rest between us on the bed.

She fills her lungs with a deep breath. "If we're going to be honest with each other–" she draws her bottom lip between her teeth, and the urge to kiss her almost makes me forget that I can't.

"You know where I come from." She pulls her shoulders up and folds her arms around her middle as if she's trying to protect herself.

It makes my protective side roar to life, and I almost pull her into my arms.

"My biggest fear is being alone," she whispers.

Fuck this.

I throw caution to the wind as I take hold of her forearm and pull her towards me. She doesn't resist as I position her against my side with her head against my shoulder. I tighten my hold on her and press a kiss to her wild hair.

She lets out a deep breath, and when her fingers tentatively brush over my chest, something tender and fragile unfurls in my chest. I should crush it, but I don't. Instead, I tuck it into the deepest part of me where it will be safe.

"You're not alone," I whisper, my voice hoarse from the affection I feel for this girl that's filling my heart.

Chapter 17

Evie

This feels too good to be wrong.

Lying in Rhett's arms, feeling his warm skin beneath my cheek, and watching his chest rise and fall with every breath he takes, wakes something inside of me. It's like a blossom on the first day of spring.

But I'm scared that the first storm will ruin it along with my heart.

I want to know more about Rhett, and lying so close to him gives me the guts to ask, "What's your favorite memory of your parents?"

He takes a deep breath and turns onto his side to face me. With my head resting on his bicep, we're so close I can feel the heat of his breath on my face.

The corner of his mouth pulls up as he remembers something, and I have to resist the urge to reach up and touch his lips. Instead, I tuck my arms between us, curling my fingers into the fabric of my shirt.

"We had this thing we always did on Sundays," he says, his voice a low rumble. "Dad would make breakfast. Well, actually, he tried. Without fail, he would burn the bacon, and I swear you could play baseball with those eggs. But we ate it without complaint." His eyes drift closed, and a sad look haunts his features. "I miss the smell of burnt bacon."

I stare at him, imprinting the image of him at this moment into my mind. This is Rhett. The sad boy who misses his dad and mom.

Intuitively, I wrap my right arm around him as I press my face into his chest. I hug him as tight as I can with my right arm. When he buries his face in my neck, and his arms lock me to him, I have to close my eyes against the tears threatening to fall for him.

That's when I know I'm in trouble. I never cry for myself, but for this man, I will weep.

Minutes pass where we hold each other.

How's it possible that you can wake up in the morning with your heart still safely in your chest, but come night, it belongs to someone else?

All it took was Rhett showing me a side of him, he keeps hidden from everyone. I've fallen in love with a little black-haired boy.

As Rhett pulls back, he brings his hand to my cheek. Our eyes meet, and it feels like there's an invisible cord tying us to each other.

What I feel for Rhett has been slowly building over the past six months. He's so easy to love. When you spend time with him, his focus is solely on you. I've never had that before. I've never meant anything to anyone.

I know I'm going to regret it in the morning, but no longer able to keep my feelings for him a secret, I whisper, "I love you."

A look of pain crosses his features, but he doesn't break eye contact with me. I don't expect him to say the words back. I meant it when I said I love him. As a friend. As a savior. As a person. Yes, I feel attracted to him, but that has nothing to do with what's in my heart.

I suppose you could say I love him the same way he cares for one of his friends.

But the moment between us shatters, and his words rain down on me like flakes of ice freezing any hope I had that he might love me back.

"You're a good friend, Evie. But that's all we can be, just friends."

I close my eyes, hiding from the truth that I'm unlovable. I turn onto my other side and force my voice to sound light.

"Night, Rhett. Thanks for letting me stay."

He takes hold of my shoulder and pulls me onto my back.

"Don't do that, Evie. Don't withdraw from me."

I keep my eyes on the other side of the room, far away from Rhett.

"I meant it as a friend," I whisper. I might as well tell him what I feel. What's the use in hiding now? "I love you as a friend. You're the first person to show me any kindness. When life turned its back on me, and I became invisible, you saw me. You take care of me without expecting anything in return. How can I not love you? You're the perfect friend."

Rhett presses his forehead against the side of my head, and his breath flutters over my ear.

"I'll always see you. I'll always take care of you. I was a dick for assuming you were confessing your undying love for me."

He pulls slightly back and cupping my cheek, he turns my face so that I'll look at him.

144

"I don't let people in easily, but once you're in, it's for life." A soft smile plays around his full lips. "From the moment I saw you, you were in here." Removing his hand from my cheek, he pats the spot over his heart.

He remains quiet for a moment before he whispers words I've never heard directed at me before.

"I love you too, Evie."

I'm hit by a tidal wave of emotions that makes my eyes brim with tears, and as Rhett offers me the safety of his chest, I'm overcome with happiness and a sense of finally belonging somewhere.

Chapter 18

Rhett

I hold Evie until she falls asleep.

Where there might have been a five percent chance of Evie and I having a romantic relationship, it's now zero. She needs someone who will take care of her and be her friend, more than she needs a horny fucker who can't keep it in his pants.

With her body tucked against mine and her steady breaths fanning over my chest, I make her a silent promise.

I'll never give up our friendship for a quick fuck with her. I'll protect her from myself.

I didn't take her seriously when she told me she loved me because, honestly, she wouldn't feel the same if I weren't taking care of her.

I think she's confusing, feeling grateful for love.

I, on the other hand, meant what I said. Evie has burrowed her way so deep into my heart there's no way of ever getting her out.

I doubt she'd like me at all if she ever finds out what a sick bastard I really am. I wonder if Evie has even had sex before.

Yeah, I'd scar her for life.

Then there's the fact that it's hard for me to trust people. As it is, I only trust Mia, Carter, and Logan.

Mom always used to say that without trust, a relationship is doomed to fail. But it's hard trusting people when you don't know whether they like you because of your money, or for who you really are inside.

Money can't buy loyalty and happiness.

With my mind full of crap, I drift off to sleep.

Waking up, the first thing I become aware of is the soft flesh beneath my fingers. Opening my eyes, I glance down, and when I see Evie's wild red curls, I let out a sigh.

Thank God, it's not some chick I fucked. I pull her body closer and bury my face in her hair, taking full advantage of the moment while she's still asleep.

147

My fingers brush over her silky skin again, and it's then I realize my hand is under her shirt. I push myself up and stare down at her.

Correction. The shirt is bundled around her ribs, giving me an eyeful of her toned stomach. Her skin is pale white compared to my tanned hand.

Unable to resist, I move my thumb back and forth, drinking in the feel of her. She lets out a breathy sigh, which makes my morning wood turn to titanium steel.

Evie starts to move, and I freeze, scared that she's going to open her eyes and bust me with my hand up her shirt. I yank my hand away and keep dead still when she turns onto her side, and throws her leg over mine.

She snuggles into my chest, curling her arm around my waist, and as she shifts her leg a little higher, her thigh brushes over my balls, nudging at my cock.

Holy fuck.

I'm going to shoot a load if she does that again.

When it's clear that she's done moving, I place my hand on the back of her neck. My fingers curl into her hair, and all I want to do is drag her up my body so I can kiss her breathless while she rides my cock.

I'm fucked.

148

I'm so fucking fucked.

Every nerve ending I have zeroes in on my cock when she shifts a little, rubbing her hot pussy against my hip while her thigh presses down on my cock.

This is fucking torture.

My hips move, slowly rolling upwards, placing a little pressure on her pussy while I get to rub my cock against her leg.

Screw that, it's not torture, it's a fucking turn on wanting something so much, but not being able to take it.

Evie's grip on me tightens, and she murmurs something ineligible.

Feeling brave that she sleeps like the dead, I move my hand down to her ass and cup her right cheek firmly.

I keep my eyes on her face as I grow a little bolder, moving my hand up to the waistband, and slipping it beneath the material. When I brush over the soft flesh of her ass cheek, I groan. She's not wearing any fucking underwear.

I'm going to come in my pants. Fuck, I want Evie so badly my cock is aching.

With my right hand, I grab a fistful of her hair and pulling her head back, I slam my mouth into hers. Digging my fingers into her ass, I pull her body over mine until she's straddling me. I can't think clearly anymore as my tongue spears into her mouth, and I taste the moan rippling up her throat.

Evie starts to kiss me back with the same hot passion. She moves her hands to my sweats and shoves them down, freeing my cock. I don't stop her as she pushes her own sweats down and positions my cock at her wet entrance. I thrust up and enter her with a loud groan...

"Rhett," she says, which isn't possible seeing as my tongue is almost down her throat. "Rhett, wake up."

Huh?

Her body disappears from on top of me, and then the fogginess of waking up intrudes on the best wet dream I've ever had.

I blink a couple of times as my hips keep rolling leisurely, and my cock brushes against the firmest ass I've ever felt.

"Rhett, you're dry humping my butt!" Evie hisses.

My eyes pop open, and my entire body moves all at once. The one second, I'm rubbing myself against Evie, and the next I'm standing at the foot of the bed with my cock straining against the sweats, ready for action.

"That must have been some dream you were having," she says teasingly, and I appreciate her making light of the moment.

"Right," I growl as I walk to the bathroom. I shut the door behind me and quickly step into the shower. The water is cold at first, and it does nothing to put out the fire burning through my veins.

With the image of Evie on top of me, I grip my cock, fantasizing that I'm thrusting into her hot pussy. It doesn't take much imagination to picture Evie naked and bouncing on my cock, which makes me shoot my load all over the wall, grinding my teeth so I won't groan out loud.

Fuck, that was intense. If that's what it's like to orgasm to a wet dream, the real thing is most probably going to kill me.

Chapter 19

Evie

I try to hide the grin on my face as I go get my clothes from the laundry room. I want to get dressed before Rhett is done showering.

Luckily I don't run into anyone, and I manage to grab my clothes and make it back to the room in a few minutes. I turn my back to the bathroom and pull the shirt off. Fastening my bra, I take a second to arrange the girls in their cups. I shove the sweatpants down and pull my panties on. When I hear the water shutting off in the bathroom, I squeak and quickly yank my dress over my head. I rush to cover myself, but the material only makes it to my waist when I hear the bathroom door open.

"Fuck," Rhett hisses behind me.

I stand frozen until I hear the bathroom door slam closed, and the water starts to run again.

My eyes grow huge when I realize Rhett is taking another shower.

Oh my, gosh! Does that mean…? Is he…?

I'm pretty sure he's masturbating in there, and it doesn't escape my attention that all it took for him to get turned on was one look at my panty-covered butt.

I finish getting dressed and giving Rhett some space, I head down to the kitchen in search of coffee.

Things have been different between Rhett and me since I spent the night at his place four months ago.

One good thing that's come out of it is that we're spending more time together, and with every passing day, I'm falling harder for him.

Since the dry humping incident, there haven't been any more intense moments between us. Rhett seems to be comfortable with only a friendship, which leaves me pining from a distance.

It's sad, really. It kills a little piece of my heart every time I see Rhett flirting with another girl. I suppose it is what it is. There's nothing I can do to change how Rhett feels about me.

Because I've been spending more time with Rhett, I've gotten to know the other guys better, as well. I've learned Carter isn't as nice as I thought he was at first, and tend to stay out of his way.

Marcus isn't much better, so I do my best to stay away from his broody glares. I'm not sure what his deal is, but it's pretty clear he's not one to be messed with.

Jaxson turned out to be surprisingly kind and funny, but I'm guessing that just like Rhett, he uses it as a wall to hide behind.

Logan is the quiet one in the group, and it's clear as daylight he only has eyes for Mia. At least they still have a chance of being together, but it's definitely not the case for Rhett and me.

I've heard about the infamous parties the guys have at their place, but this will be my first time going to one. I asked Willow to come with me, but she already has plans to go home for the weekend, which is a bummer. It would've been nice to have her there with me.

Since Willow's moved in, it's been heaven. I never knew how amazing it could be sharing a home with another girl. She's so easy to get along with. It was the most natural thing to fall into a friendship with her.

154

Although it's spring, the nights are still pretty nippy. I'm standing in front of my closet trying to decide what I should wear when Willow walks into my room and comes to stand beside me.

All my clothes are practical. I don't know what would be fitting to wear to my first party.

"Girl, we need to do something about this wardrobe you've got going," Willow says, with a mock look of tortured furrowing her brow. "This is a fashion disaster."

"Geez, don't hold back on account of my feelings," I tease, bumping my shoulder against hers.

"My hands are itching to take it all and to transform it into pieces that won't hurt my eyes."

I smile as I glance at her. "I wouldn't mind. I've seen your clothes. I'm not too proud to admit that I suck when it comes to fashion."

"You don't suck," she says, throwing her arm over my shoulder to give me a sideways hug. "You just need a push in the right direction."

"I don't know what to wear tonight," I admit, biting my lower lip. I want to look pretty for Rhett.

Willow begins to look through my closet, her face scrunching with every single thing she doesn't like. I'm about to lose hope when her face brightens up. She yanks out a pair of cut-off shorts I bought but haven't had the guts to wear. Plus, it's been cold.

Shoving it against my chest, she says, "Hold this. I'll be right back."

I stare at the shorts with huge eyes thinking how I'm going to freeze my butt off tonight.

Willow comes whirling back into my room, carrying a pair of caramel knee-high boots with an off-shoulder semi-sheer knit sweater. I'm hoping it will keep me warm.

"Come on, get your sexy ass in those shorts. When I'm done with you, you're going to make heads turn."

I strip out of the sweats and baggy shirt I'm wearing and drag on the shorts.

"Cute undies," Willow remarks, making me blush furiously.

I'm a comfort kinda gal, and boyshorts are my go-to preference.

Her eyes lock onto my bra, which is pretty dull. "Take off the bra, you won't need it."

My eyes widen, but I finish zipping up the shorts, then take off the bra.

156

She hands me the sweater, and the moment I have it on, Willow pulls the collar down my left shoulder. She makes a couple of tweaks here and there until she's satisfied. I love the sleeves, which cover half my hands with a thick cuff.

Next are the boots, and luckily they're cozy and warm. Taking hold of my shoulder, Willow steers me over to the dresser and pushes me down on the chair.

She starts to work with the rat nest on top of my head, and all I can do is stare at how beautiful her hands are as they flutter around my head.

I'm stunned by the final result when she says, "Yep, you're going to have all the guys drooling."

She's piled most of my curls on top of my head in a messy bun, which I can never get right. Mine always ends up looking like a blob. Loose curls hang to my shoulders, but the majority of my neck is exposed.

"Now for your makeup, then you're all set to go." Willow doesn't go overboard like I expected she would. She only brushes on some eye shadow, mascara, and rounds the look off with rustic lip stain.

She used a dark, shimmery eyeshadow, and it makes the green of my eyes pop. With the rustic coloring on my lips, my skin looks snowy and soft.

157

Hell, even I have to admit I look pretty, and it makes me feel good.

"My job here is done," Willow says as she stands back to admire her work. "I'll see you on Sunday night. Have fun tonight and don't do anything I wouldn't do."

I get up and give her a hug. "Enjoy your weekend, and thank you for making me look pretty."

Hugging me back, she says, "You've always been pretty, Evie. I've just added a few touches."

We let go of each other, and walking Willow to the door, I say, "When you get back will you teach me a few tricks?"

"Sure, it will be so much fun." She opens the front door but then looks back at me from over her shoulder. "On second thought, do everything I wouldn't do, then you can tell me all about your wild night when I get back."

I laugh and shake my head because we both know I don't have a wild bone in my body.

After Willow leaves, I spray on some deodorant, grab a coat in case it gets colder tonight, and head over to Rhett's.

The front door is open when I get to the house. I'm thirty minutes early because I'm hoping to spend some time with Rhett before everyone arrives, and maybe I can help with setting things up for the party.

Hearing voices coming from the kitchen, I walk in that direction. I drape my coat over the back of the couch and leave my bag on the seat.

As I walk into the kitchen, Marcus says, "Dude, I'm beating you, hands down."

Rhett chuckles as he places red solo cups next to a keg of beer.

"Only by four screws," Rhett says. "By the end of tonight, the figures will change."

"Yeah, which means you'll be further behind," Marcus laughs.

I walk closer to see what the guys are so engrossed with. They're standing around Marcus, staring at his laptop screen. When I get close enough, I peek under Carter's arm, and I see the words *Screw Crew Wall Of Fame* as a heading to what seems to be a list of names.

It takes me a moment to put it all together.

The guys made a list of girls they have slept with.

I shouldn't be surprised after running into Rhett and that girl, Josie, at the library a couple of months back. After all, she had just given him a blowjob.

But still... There's a painful twinge in my chest, and I'm once again reminded I actually have very little in common with Rhett and his friends.

I'm about to sneak out before the guys notice I'm here, to avoid an awkward situation, but then Jaxson turns around and his eyes land on me.

He lets out a long wolf whistle and says, "Damn, Evie, you look smoking."

I fist my hands, digging my fingers into the cuffs of the sweater and feel myself blush all the way to the roots of my hair.

Rhett knocks over a tower of solo cups as he swings around. His eyes widen, and his lips part as a burst of air explodes over them.

When the rest of the guys turn to look at me, things start to feel really awkward at the speed of light.

Logan clears his throat before excusing himself. Marcus doesn't hide the fact that he's blatantly checking me out, his eyes sweeping over every inch of me.

"What the fuck are you wearing?" Rhett growls, yanking my attention back to him. Where he looked stunned a second ago, and I was hoping he would notice the effort Willow and I put into my appearance, it evaporates as dread coils in my stomach.

"Let's give them some privacy," Carter says, immediately heading for the door. Jaxson and Marcus follow right behind him. I get a feeling they're all too willing to throw me to the wolf so they can save their own butts and not get caught in the line of fire.

I swallow hard as Rhett's eyes sweep over me, before stopping at my chest.

"You're not wearing a bra," he hisses, and the pissed off look turns murderous.

I take a step backward, so I'm closer to the door in case I need to make a quick escape.

I'm going to stand up for myself, though. Just because Rhett doesn't like what I'm wearing doesn't mean I look bad. After all, Jaxson thinks I'm smoking, which I assume is his way of saying I look hot.

"Our deal was that you keep your clothes on," Rhett bites out.

Feeling hurt, I wrap my arms around my chest and hunch my shoulders.

"You don't have to be so rude," I whisper. "I get that you think I look awful."

I'm about to turn around and leave when anger bubbles to life in my chest.

I straighten my spine and scowl at Rhett. "You know what," I snap, lifting my chin, "I actually think I look pretty."

Rhett's eyebrows pop into his hairline, and he stalks towards me. He pinches some of my sweater between his thumb and forefinger, pulling it away from my chest.

Glaring down at me, he hisses, "Where the fuck is the other half of this outfit? I can see your fucking nipples! I don't pay you to look like a whore."

He lets go of my sweater as if it's burning him, and I immediately cross my arms over my breasts.

I felt pretty and confident when I left my apartment, but now I feel cheap and exposed. I can't believe he just said that to me. Anger and shame wars inside of me as disappointment starts to weigh down on my shoulders.

There's so much I can say to hurt him back, but that's not who I am. I shake my head lightly and turning my back on Rhett, I rush out of the kitchen. I grab my coat and quickly put it on before snatching my bag off the seat. On my way out of the front door, I shrug on my coat and fasten every button so I can cover the outfit.

"Evie!" Rhett hollers behind me.

I've had more than enough insults to last me a lifetime, and I sure as hell can't handle anymore. I break out into a run so I can get away from that house and the man who just broke my heart.

Chapter 20

Rhett

I'm about to go after Evie, when Carter grabs hold of my arm, holding me back.

"Let her go," he says with anger written all over his face.

Logan is standing at the bottom of the stairs, with a look of disappointment.

I open my mouth but swallow my protest when Carter's face turns dark.

"You were out of line, Rhett. Give Evie time. I think you've done enough damage for one night."

I yank my arm out of Carter's hold and turn to face him. "Stay out of this."

"Rhett, you need to calm down," Logan says as he comes to stand next to Carter.

Seeing my best friends upset with me brings it home, and it makes shame and disappointment bubble in my chest.

What have I done?

The thought sweeps through me like a storm, pissing on the fire that was feeding my rage.

How could I say those things to Evie? What the fuck came over me?

Her perky nipples, that's what.

Seeing her dressed like that unleashed something far worse than the perverted monster that's been living inside of me. This was possessive and dominant.

It made me see red, knowing my friends could see every sexy part of her body I was seeing. Her toned legs, and those boots… fuck those boots. Her slim neck and slender shoulders. Her smoky eyes and red lips. I wanted to bite those lips until they were naturally red and swollen.

She looked like sex in boots, and the domineering jerk inside of me was roaring with jealousy.

Logan reaches out and gives my shoulder a comforting squeeze, but his words are the opposite. "You called Evie a whore." Logan being upset is a huge deal. It takes a lot to ruffle his feathers, and right now, he's far from happy with me. "Evie ate out of dumpsters to avoid selling herself for food. Honestly, I don't think you can repair the damage you've done."

Hearing the hard truth from Logan makes my body shudder with dread.

Have I fucked up things between Evie and me and ruined our friendship?

Knowing Carter and Logan are right, I walk back into the house. I only make it to the living room when my phone vibrates in my pocket. I take it out and unlock the screen.

I'm confused when I see a message from Evie.

Evie: I've paid everything I've managed to save over the last few months to your bank account. It's all I have right now. I'll repay the rest of what I owe as quick as I can.

It feels as if the ground gives way beneath my feet as I read the message again and again.

She's going to run!

Fuck.

The thought has my body moving so fast, and I'm out the front door before Carter or Logan can stop me. I have to make things right before I lose her.

That's if you haven't lost her already, dumbass!

I jump in my car and make it to Evie's place in record time. Running up to her apartment, I knock on the door, but when she doesn't open, I start to panic.

166

She couldn't have packed everything so fast? It's only been twenty minutes since I last saw her.

Pulling my keys from my pocket, I look for the spare key to her apartment. I never thought I'd have to use it. I only kept it in case she locked herself out.

It's another dick move on my part, intruding on her privacy, but I have to see her and make things right.

I let myself in, shutting the door behind me before I walk to Evie's room.

The sweater, shorts, and boots are lying in a heap in the middle of her room. Hearing water running, I walk to the bathroom, and when I see Evie, relief floods me.

I'm in time to stop her. Thank God.

Evie splashes water on her face then grabs a towel, and as she dries her face, she starts to walk towards me.

"Hey," I say so she won't bump into me.

She lets out a piercing shriek, throws the towel at me, and stumbles back. Her face pales from the fright, and she loses her balance. I rush forward, but I'm too late, and I watch with horror how Evie's butt hits the floor, and the back of her head collides with the bath. The sound is sickening and scary, making me drop to my knees beside Evie.

She groans as she reaches for the back of her head.

"I'm sorry," I whisper and sliding my hand behind her neck, I pulling her forward so I can check if there's blood. With her hair still piled up on her head, it makes the task easier. Luckily there's no blood, only a goose egg that's already forming.

Positioning one arm behind her back, and another under her knees, I lift her to my chest as I climb to my feet.

She weighs next to nothing as I carry her to the bed, and it only makes my protective side rear its ugly head. Once I've set her down, I rush to the kitchen to grab a bag of frozen vegetables from her freezer. When I get back to her bedroom, I sit down beside her and gently press the frozen bag to the back of her head.

She takes it from me and moves away, putting plenty of space between us.

"What are you doing here?" she says softly, sounding worn out.

I know it won't be easy to fix what I've broken, but I'm determined to try.

"I came to apologize," I say, turning my body to face her.

I wish I could take her hand, but she's closed off, and her walls are back up.

She doesn't say anything as she stares at the floor.

Needing her to look at me, I hook a finger under her chin and turn her face to me. I see red blemishes around her eyes, and it's evidence of just how much I hurt her.

"I was a dick, Evie."

She pulls her face away from my hand. "Can we talk tomorrow? I want to be alone right now."

Her words are a punch to my gut. Evie's biggest fear is being alone, and she'd rather face that than have me here.

She drops the frozen bag on the floor, and when she gets up and walks over to her closet, it sinks in that she's only wearing boyshorts and a flimsy tank top.

Instead of staring at her ass, my eyes are drawn back to her face, washed clean of makeup. The evidence of her tears makes me feel guilt-ridden as fuck.

I've kept my distance from Evie because she's so innocent, and I didn't want to corrupt her with my depravity. How she managed to remain pure with the past she's had to deal with, goes beyond my understanding.

Evie is as decent as they come, and I called her a whore.

I wait while she drags on a pair of sweats and a t-shirt. When she's done, she lets out a tired sigh as she finally lifts her eyes to mine.

"Say what you have to say so you can go, Rhett."

I would've been able to handle her anger, but the hollowness in her voice guts me even further.

She just wants me gone.

I stand up and take a deep breath, needing to make her understand that I didn't mean it.

"You looked beautiful tonight. I lost my shit because of it. I didn't want any of the guys seeing you like that, because I knew they would see what I've known all along. You're drop-dead gorgeous inside and out. I was scared one of them would do what I was too chicken shit to do."

Well, I wasn't planning on laying my heart out in front of her, but now that I've said it, there's no taking it back.

She just stares at me, and it's making my stomach tighten with nerves.

Please don't tell me to fuck off.

I send up the silent prayer as I wait for her to say something.

170

When she looks down at her feet and tucks some of the curls behind her ear, my body tenses as I wait for her to tell me she'll never forgive me.

"The day I went to live with Eric and Charlotte, I thought I was the luckiest girl in the world. I finally had a family who wanted me. I had a home where I could be a part of something bigger than myself."

It's not what I expected to hear, and it takes my mind a moment to catch-up.

"It only took me a few days to realize nothing was as it seemed. The kids didn't laugh, and everyone would tense up whenever Eric or Charlotte walked into a room. At first, I was on kitchen duty, but a few months later, one of the older girls left, and I took over doing the laundry."

I'm not sure where Evie is going with this story, but I listen greedily because it's about her past. It's something new I'm getting to learn about her.

"Some of the loads were the usual stuff, clothes I saw everyone wear daily. But there were loads filled with lingerie and some –"

She takes a deep breath and wraps her arms around her. She shrugs as she glances up at me, an unsettled look in her eyes.

My heart starts to beat faster, and my gut tightens. This isn't just a memory Evie's sharing with me. Something happened, and I made it worse.

She clears her throat and drops her eyes to my chest. "There was blood on the clothes. Charlotte brought the soiled loads and took the clean ones, and I knew better than to ask her where the blood came from. I suppose I was trying to protect myself from whatever was happening. If I didn't know the truth, it couldn't hurt me. Just before I turned eighteen, Eric and Charlotte sat me down. I was told that I would start working at the ranch on my birthday."

My breaths come faster, and when she takes too long to continue, I rasp, "What happens at the ranch?"

"You become a sex worker."

I close my eyes, wishing I could take back what I said to Evie.

"That's why I ran," she whispers. "I couldn't imagine anything worse than being forced to have sex with multiple men every night."

I take a step towards her, but catch myself in time. I'm not sure she wants me touching her right now.

"I'm sorry, Evie. I didn't mean it. I was jealous," I say urgently, praying she'll believe me.

Her eyes find mine, and she pins me with a determined look.

"I'm not a whore, Rhett. I've never sold my body for sex. I might have cleaned houses topless, but the worst that makes me is a stripper. There's a huge difference. I never performed a sexual act for money. I never will. I don't care if men stare at me. Their eyes can't hurt me."

I open my mouth, but she quickly holds her hand up to silence me.

"I feel violated. You think by throwing money my way, I'm your property. I'm not. I never will be. I'm not a whore, Rhett. I'm definitely not *your* whore."

"I never said you were *my* whore," I say lamely.

"You treated me like one," she whispers, but she might as well be screaming the words at me. "You've done it twice now. I'm grateful that you stepped in to help me when I had no one, but it doesn't mean I have no self-respect. It doesn't mean you can disrespect me. I might have been eating out of dumpsters," her voice breaks, and a tear sneaks down her face, "but I'm not trash."

When her face crumbles, I can't just stand and watch her anymore. I shoot forward, and before she can move away, I wrap my arms around her. I hold her tightly as she breaks down. I want to kiss her pain away, but instead, I offer her the comfort of my chest.

"I'm so fucking sorry, Evie," I whisper into her hair. "I never meant to make you feel like that."

Now that I know more about Evie's past, it makes my protective side grow into something dark.

I've always been protective of Mia, but I've never felt anything like this before. Knowing Logan would take care of Mia, whenever I couldn't, gave me peace of mind.

But Evie only has me. She's been hurt, scared, and abandoned. The need in me to shield her from whatever life will still throw her way, becomes a living, breathing force.

I press a kiss to the top of her head, then bringing my hands to her face, and framing her cheeks, I lean down, I catch her eyes. "Since I've met you, all I've wanted to do was protect you. Tonight, I was a dick, and I hurt you. I'll regret it for the rest of my life. I love you, Evie. I fucking love you. There's so much good in you; it makes me feel half decent whenever I'm around you. I have my fucked-up issues, and they got out of control tonight. It won't happen again."

The hurt doesn't disappear from her eyes, and honestly, I didn't expect it to. But when she nods, I feel the tight hold on my gut loosen a bit.

Chapter 21

Evie

"You wanna go back to the party?" Rhett asks.

I pull my face free from his hands and shake my head.

"No, I'm just going to go to sleep," I whisper as I walk to the bathroom for some toilet paper. I wipe the tears from my cheeks and blow my nose before heading back to the room.

"Can I stay with you?" Rhett asks.

I sit down on the bed and think about what he just asked me. Part of me wants to put as much distance as possible between us, so Rhett will never be able to hurt me again like he did tonight. But then there's my heart, my foolish, forgiving heart that loves Rhett.

With my mind screeching no and my heart yelling, yes, I nod.

I get up and pull the covers back. I usually sleep in my boyshorts and tank top, but seeing as Rhett is spending the night, I keep my sweatpants on.

I pull the t-shirt off and duck under the covers.

Rhett switches the light off, and I watch his profile as he pulls his shirt over his head. When he steps out of his jeans, I divert my eyes even though I can't see much in the dark.

He climbs into bed, and when he reaches for me, I let him pull me to his side. I rest my cheek on the warm skin over his heart and wrap an arm around his waist.

His one hand disappears into my hair, and I'm not sure what he's doing until he unties it.

"That's better." His voice is a low rumble in the dark.

We lie in silence for a couple of minutes, then Rhett asks, "Don't you wonder about your biological parents?"

"No," I answer honestly. "They didn't want me."

He presses his lips to my forehead, and keeping them there, he whispers, "I want you."

I smile into the dark and wrap my arm tighter around Rhett.

Two years later.

Every time I think I can't handle more, the universe takes it as a dare.

A week ago, I walked in on Rhett having sex. I don't know which part of the whole painful experience hurt most. Seeing him naked with another girl, or the fact that she has red hair like me.

It's no secret that if it has a pulse, Rhett will sleep with it. But actually seeing him thrusting into another girl… that just about killed me.

Even though Rhett tells me often that he loves me, I've only said the words to him twice. The first time was the year we met, and I meant it as a friend. The second time was last year, but then I meant I loved him with all my heart.

Rhett says he doesn't see anything more than friendship between us, but when he holds me as if he's scared I'll vanish before his eyes, it makes me wonder. He looks at me as if I'm the most beautiful thing he's ever laid eyes on, and sometimes he even flirts with me, but nothing ever comes from it.

"It's time for me to let you go," I whisper to the dark. I'm only hurting myself by staying here and holding onto a hope that will never materialize into something more.

I can't be around Rhett without my heart breaking every day. It's becoming an endless cycle.

I glance back at the cab that's waiting to take me to the bus station and suck in a deep breath before I walk to the front door.

Usually, I just walk inside, but tonight I knock on the door.

I hear laughter inside, and when Rhett opens the door, and he sees it's me, he frowns.

"Why are you knocking? Come in."

I take a few steps backward and shove my hands into the pockets of my jacket.

Rhett tilts his head to the side, and he takes a step towards me, which only makes me take another one backward. I need to keep the space between us.

I force my eyes to stay locked with his, as I say the words I've repeated over and over to myself the past week.

"I want you to know how thankful I am for everything you've done for me. I'll never forget it."

The spit in my mouth thickens, and I swallow hard.

The questioning look on Rhett's face turns to shock as he catches on to what I'm doing.

My heartbeat speeds up until it's slamming against my ribs, trying to free itself from my body so it can stay behind with Rhett.

"I'm leaving. I've come to say goodbye," I whisper, unable to say the words much louder.

"You're leaving?" he breathes. His face turns hard, and it looks as if it has been chiseled out of stone. "Why?"

I owe him honesty. It's the least I can do after everything he's done for me.

"Loving you hurts too much. Seeing you with other women and knowing they're getting the one thing I want most, is killing me. I'm in love with you, Rhett. I want it all. I want you, and I'm not prepared to share you with anyone else. But I know you don't feel the same way about me, and that's why I have to leave."

Pain flashes across his face, and I hate that I'm hurting him. Because I'm a selfish coward, I'm running away. It's what I do best.

Before I can lose my nerve, I dart forward and give him a quick hug and kiss on the cheek. He's so stunned that I manage to pull away before he can take hold of me.

"I love you, Rhett Daniels. You'll always be my hero," I choke the words out before I turn around and run for the cab.

"Evie!" He yells after me.

I climb into the back of the cab as fast as I can, and scream, "Go! Drive!" The cab starts to pull away, and I look back to Rhett as he comes running towards us. I can't hold the tears in any longer, and I let them fall as I place my hand flat against the window. "I love you so much," I whisper as I watch him stop in the middle of the road. His hands fly to the back of his head, and the look on his face is pure devastation. "It's for the best, Evie," I whisper to myself, wiping my tears away with the back of my hand.

The ride to the bus station is a blur of heartache. I somehow manage to pay the right fee for both the cab and the bus ticket. I pick a random destination, Los Angeles. I've read the weather is perfect there.

The thirty minutes I spend waiting for the bus, I keep glancing around, scared Rhett will show up and convince me to stay. It wouldn't take much effort on his part.

When it comes to Rhett, it's so easy to forgive him.

But I have to do this for me.

Chapter 22

Rhett

Six years later.

I'm watching *Frozen* for the hundredth time with Danny tucked into my side. She's rubbing a piece of my shirt between her thumb and forefinger, her eyes glued to the screen.

When the movie gets close to our part, she scrambles to her knees and wildly slaps at my chest.

"Get ready, Uncle Ledge!"

I watch her take a deep breath, and I start to sing along with her to the soundtrack. I watch her little face as she concentrates on getting the words right.

Her voice gets stronger as we near the chorus, and when I scoop her into my arms and dart up from the couch, she squeals with laughter. I spin her around the living room while we both shout at the tops of our lungs, "Let it go. Let it go. Can't hold it back anymore."

By the time the song is finished, I'm out of breath. I fall back on the couch, and Danny snuggles into my side again.

We continue to watch the movie as if we didn't just dance and shout like a couple of crazy people a couple of seconds ago.

As the credits start to roll, Danny looks up at me. "When are you going to find your Elsa, Uncle Ledge?"

I'm not about to ruin Danny's little romantic heart, so I reply, "I've already found my Anna, but right now, she's having an adventure."

Danny claps her hands. "Oh, you like Elsa's sister. Ooooh. I can't wait until she's back, and she can tell me all about it."

The smile fades from my face, and I whisper, "You and me both, Princess."

I told Danny I found my Anna because the character reminds me more of Evie than Elsa does. It was the easiest way I could think to explain it to Danny.

I sit and watch as Danny falls asleep before I slowly get up and cover her with the Little Mermaid blanket lying over the back of the couch.

On my way to join the gang where they're barbecuing, I grab a beer from the fridge. I pop the cap off and take a sip as I step outside.

"Did she finally fall asleep?" Della asks, looking tired as hell where she's sitting with Christopher sleeping on her lap. His one leg is up against her chest.

"Let me take him so you can have a breather," I say, setting down my beer and picking up my godson.

"I swear, if it weren't for you, I'd be crazy by now," Getting up, Della stretches before she presses a kiss to my cheek and walks towards the house.

"Della, where are you going?" Carter yells from where he's standing by the barbeque with Jaxson, Marcus, and Ryan.

"I'm going to go pee before my bladder explodes," she yells back at him.

"Please grab me a beer on the way back."

Della glares at him before she disappears inside the house. I take a seat by Miss Sebastian, Mia, Willow, and Leigh.

"She wouldn't let me take Christopher," Miss Sebastian whispers to me. "She was waiting for you to come outside." The smile on Miss Sebastian's face tells me she's not upset about it, but instead proud of me.

185

Then she adds, "If I could have kids, I'd only trust you with them as well."

As Della comes back outside, I smile when I see the beer in her hand. She waves it in the air. "Come fetch your drink."

Carter comes over, but instead of going to Della, he heads in my direction.

"How's my little-man doing?"

"Carter Hayes," Della snaps. "Don't you dare touch Christopher. I just got him to sleep."

"But, you handed him to Rhett?" Carter says with a look of confusion.

"Because he's the only other person whose arms our children will sleep in. The second you touch them, they wake up and then I have to start all over again."

I smirk at Carter as he takes the beer from Della.

Then I start to smell something just as Christopher begins to wiggle in my arms.

"Oh, hell no. Take your kid," I say as I dart up and pass him to Carter. "I draw the line at changing diapers."

I take a few steps back, almost falling over the chair I was sitting on, and it makes everyone burst out laughing.

"Scared of getting your hands dirty?" Miss Sebastian teases me.

By the time I get back to the hotel, I'm exhausted. Mia and Logan offered that I stay with them, but as much as I love my niece, I don't want to be woken by her crying every couple of hours.

I rented out my place in New York when I moved to LA. Everyone thinks it's because I wanted to help Jaxson and Marcus set up the new business, but it's because Evie is there. I haven't seen or spoken to her in... fuck... has it really been six years? Damn, I last saw her when I was twenty-two. I turned twenty-eight last month. But, it still feels like yesterday.

Marcus tends to drop something about Evie here and there, and it's pathetic how I've become dependent on him just so I know what's happening in her life.

It's small stuff.

'I hear Evie's doing okay.'

'Evie's still single.'

He'll whisper it when walking past me, or while we're getting coffee in the mornings. I'll just nod, so he knows I've heard him.

If I were half the man I claim to be, I'd be knocking on her door and making her mine.

But I'm not the man everyone thinks I am.

I've become the man I used to warn Mia about. I spend my Saturdays at an exclusive club where I fuck random strangers. Lately, even that's starting to lose its appeal.

With all my friends settled down, I'm forced to face the horrible truth that I'm alone because I let the only woman I'll ever love walk out of my life.

Chapter 23

Evie

Taking a cab to work, I stare out the window, not really seeing anything.

While Willow was staying with me, things were going well, but since she moved in with Marcus, my life started to slowly crumble around me. Not that I had much to begin with.

I've been saving every cent so I can repay Rhett Daniels. It took much longer than I had hoped it would, but when I get paid tomorrow, I'll be able to transfer the full amount he gave me to his bank account. Then I just have to save the interest and repay him that, as well. I won't owe anyone anything after that.

The cab stops outside the restaurant where I work as a waitress. I pay the fee with a heavy heart, wishing I could move closer to work, so I didn't have to waste money on transport. That will never happen, though. The apartments in this part of town are way too costly.

I walk around the back of the building and go in via the staff entrance. Keeping my head down, I don't greet anyone as I walk to the restroom. Stripping out of my clothes, I fold it all neatly before putting it in my bag. I remove my apron from where it's hanging against the wall and tie it around my waist.

Yeah, this is what my life has come to. I'm a waitress in a nude restaurant where the uniform is only a black apron and black heels.

I chuckle bitterly as I wonder what Rhett would think if he could see me now. He tried to save me from this life, but in the end, I ran from him and right back into the clutches of poverty.

"At least you're not selling your body," my heart whispers.

"Yeah, right. Keep lying to yourself. What you're doing is no better than being a whore," my mind sneers.

I've let my hair grow, and thankfully it reaches past my nipples. Some of the other girls complained when they saw I was covering myself, but management likes the idea of my breasts playing peek-a-boo with their elite clientele.

I place my bag in my locker, then go grab a notepad and pen. As I scribble on the paper to make sure the pen is working, I push through the massive double doors leading to the restaurant.

The cold air hits me like it always does, and I shiver. The AC is set low to make our nipples hard.

When I get to my section, the girl who was working the shift before me heads into the back. I scan my section, assessing the customers I'll be serving.

A man catches my eyes, nodding subtly. I walk over to his table, swinging my hips for extra effect. It helps with the tips if you put on a show for them.

"What can I get for you, Sir?" I ask, forcing my voice to come out sweetly.

"Get me a refill," he barks at me before turning back to his much younger date with a leering smile.

Pig. I note his table number then go look on the computer to see what he's having to drink before placing his order at the bar.

I'm waiting while the bartender fixes the drink when someone nudges me lightly against the shoulder.

Glancing to the side, I see that it's Kyle, the owner's son.

"How's my favorite waitress doing?" he asks, turning on the charm.

"I'm well, thank you. For how long are you home this time?" I ask.

Kyle loves to travel. I only see him when he comes home once in a while. So far, he's been nothing but sweet to me, and he doesn't ogle my body like every other man in this establishment does.

"Actually, I'm going to be helping out here for a while. My dad is taking my mom on a cruise."

"Oh, that's nice." The bartender sets the tumbler down in front of me. I place it on a tray and lifting it, I say, "Welcome back. I'll see you around."

When I start to walk away, Kyle quickly catches up to me.

"Have dinner with me after work?" He grins, and I have to admit, he is attractive. It would also be nice to be wined and dined. I haven't been on a date in ages.

"I get off at three in the morning, Kyle. It's way past dinner time then," I tease.

I take another step forward, and this time he lightly touches my elbow.

"Have an early morning breakfast with me then," he tries again.

Admiring him for being persistent, I decide to agree. What do I have to lose?

"Okay. I'll see you at three."

His smile warms his whole face. With his blonde hair and blue eyes, Kyle is a huge hit with the ladies.

After ten o'clock, the kitchen closes, and a DJ starts to play more upbeat music. I stay busy taking drink orders until after two in the morning when it finally begins to slow down. A few die-hards hang around until the bartender rings a bell, announcing we'll be closing in thirty minutes.

The last ten minutes drag out endlessly, and it feels as if my toes are being ground to a pulp in the heels.

When the last customer gets up to leave, I head to the restroom. Once inside, I kick off the shoes and groan as I curl my toes against the cool tiles.

"It's heavenly, right?" One of the other waitresses says as she's busy buttoning her shirt.

I nod before I walk over to my locker and take my bag from it. I get dressed fast, then spend a minute washing my hands a couple of times. I chuck the heels in my locker and hang my apron on its peg.

All I want to do is go home and sleep, but I've already agreed to the date with Kyle.

As I leave the restroom, Kyle straightens from where he was leaning against the wall. "Hey, beautiful," he murmurs, taking a step closer to me. Without the heels on, I only reach his shoulder. His eyes wander over my face, then he surprises me when he says, "You look tired. How about I take a rain check on breakfast, and instead give you a ride home?"

The first thought that pops into my mind is I don't want Kyle to see where I live. He's used to only having the best in life.

He must see the hesitation on my face, because he quickly adds, "I know where you live, Evie. I've seen your personnel file."

"You've looked at my file?" I ask with a frown forming on my forehead.

He laughs nervously, just realizing how stalkerish it sounds. "I looked at it because I'm taking over for six months. I'll admit I might have stared way too long at the photo on your application."

His honesty makes me feel better, and I smile to set him at ease.

"So, can I give you a ride home?" he asks again, giving me a hopeful look.

"Sure," I relent. It will save me the cab fee.

"Let's go." When he takes hold of my hand, I quickly glance around us. I don't want any of the other staff to see I'm leaving with Kyle. They'll think I'm sleeping with the boss' son for an ulterior motive.

When we reach his car, he opens the passenger door for me. I get in, and instantly, I feel intimidated by all the wealth. You can smell the leather.

When Kyle climbs in behind the wheel, he smiles at me before starting the car. For the first couple of minutes, we drive in silence. It's comfortable and puts me at ease.

"I've wanted to ask you out for a while now," Kyle admits when he stops at a red light.

Surprised, I glance at him, not knowing what to say.

"Just to be clear, I don't care that you work for my father. I'd like a chance to date you."

He's so straightforward it's actually refreshing. There are no secrets for me to try and figure out.

When I continue to keep quiet, he glances at me before pulling away as the light turns green.

"I guess I'm asking if you'll date me, Evie?"

Finally, I find my voice, "I'm not sure I understand what you're asking."

A playful smile spreads across his face as he reaches for my hand.

"I'm asking whether you'll date me exclusively."

My eyes widen. "Are you asking me to be your girlfriend?"

"Yeah," he laughs.

"Don't you think we should get to know each other better first?" This is happening way too fast.

Nevermind that, I've never had a boyfriend before. I wouldn't know what to do with him.

"By dating, we'll get to know each other," he makes a valid point.

I stare at his profile for a while, considering his question. It wouldn't be a hardship to date Kyle. He has manners, and there is the added bonus that he's quite handsome.

"Okay," I agree, willing to give it a try.

When he parks outside my building, I take the seat belt off. As I reach for the door, Kyle leans over the console and framing my face with his hands, he presses his mouth to mine.

I'm so shocked that I freeze at first. The kiss is slow and tentative, but as I start to relax, Kyle deepens it by parting my lips with his tongue. The second I taste him, I feel a fluttering in my stomach. I give myself over to the kiss, enjoying the touch of a man for the first time in a way too many years.

When he pulls back, he whispers, "Now we have the first kiss out of the way. Can I pick you up before work and take you to dinner?"

I nod, not yet trusting my voice.

"I'll pick you up at five. That way, we'll have enough time before your shift starts."

"Okay," I whisper.

He gets out of the car and walks me to my door where he kisses me again, but this time it's quick.

"Sweet dreams, Evie," he whispers as he lets go of me and takes a step back.

"Night, Kyle," I say. I watch him walk away before I walk into the building. Entering my apartment, I don't bother switching on any lights. I head straight to the bathroom and take a quick shower before climbing into bed.

As I snuggle into my pillow, a slow smile spreads across my face. Maybe things will start going my way from now on.

Chapter 24

Rhett

I frown as I stare at the notification from the bank. I wasn't expecting any money.

I shoot a quick email to my banker, asking him to check where the money came from before I shove the phone back in my pocket.

I got back to LA yesterday. I couldn't believe how much work was waiting for me at the office. You leave for three days, and the place collapses.

It's only after nine when I finally leave the office. Thankfully, Marcus will be back at the office tomorrow, which will help a lot.

I scroll through my messages as I walk to my car. Not seeing anything that requires my urgent attention, I shove the phone in my pocket. Climbing in my car, I make my way home. Tonight I just want to enjoy a beer before I head to bed.

When I stop at a red light, I glance around the area. I notice the neon word Marilyn's. The windows are blacked out, so I can't see inside. I'll Google the place when I get home. Funny how I've driven past it a hundred times, but I only notice it now.

When I get home, I throw my keys on the counter and grab a beer from the fridge. I plop down on the couch and kick off my shoes before I rest my feet on the coffee table. Yanking my tie loose, I take a deep pull from the bottle.

Fuck, yeah. Now, this is much better.

I finish half of the beer before I pull my phone out so I can check my emails. I delete a couple before I see the one from my banker.

Opening it, I scan the details of the funds I received earlier.

Payee: E. Cole

E. Cole? The only E. Cole I know, is Evie.

It takes a moment for my mind to play catch up with what my eyes are seeing.

A tornado of emotions sweeps through my chest as the shock slams into my gut.

Evie paid me back every cent I gave her.

I gave her that fucking money!

I rise to my feet and place the bottle on the coffee table, so I don't throw the damn thing. I drop my phone on the couch and fist my hands.

My thoughts are a jumbled mess. I start stalking the length of my living room, trying to process the information. My emotions keep switching from anger to astonishment, giving me fucking whiplash.

Evie paid me back.

I stop in the middle of the living room as my mind clears, and two distinct thoughts stand out.

Evie is still thinking of me.

She had to have at least thought of me once a month as she was saving the funds. She never forgot about me like I thought.

For Evie, it never was about the money.

That means she really meant it when she said she loved me.

Fuck!

From the moment I met Evie, money played a prominent role in our relationship. I couldn't let my guard down around her even though I loved her. I was a stupid dumbass back then. I've let the best thing that's ever happened to me slip through my fingers because I have fucked-up trust issues.

Well, there is the tiny problem of the perverted secret I have, but it pales in comparison to the fact that I never trusted Evie.

Fuck, I was so caught up in myself she didn't stand a chance.

What the hell have I done to Evie, to me... to us?

Every day she was in my life, I was waiting for her to walk out on me. When she did, it solidified what I thought I had known all along. I was nothing but a free ride to her.

But that never was the case.

And now...

It's not about the actual money, but instead, what it all signifies. That I was an asshole who broke my promise of protecting Evie, even from myself. All because I couldn't see the truth, my heart knew all along.

Evie wasn't like the other girls. She really cared for me.

But it's been six years.

A lot has happened. Fuck, Evie could've changed. Look at the guys, they're all settled and happy. I'm the only fucker who's still stuck in the past.

But she might still be the Evie I knew and fell in love with. If there's a chance that she still feels something for me, don't I owe it to us to find out?

The least I can do is apologize to her for being a dick and not trusting her.

"Don't rush into this," I whisper.

"Fuck."

I shake my head at myself.

"You're totally going to rush into this balls first."

I grin at myself as I start to think of ways I can worm my way back into Evie's life.

Chapter 25

Evie

Kyle and I have been dating for a couple of weeks now, and I can't remember the last time I was this happy. He's the perfect gentleman and goes out of his way to make me feel special.

I'm starting to fall in love with him.

Last night, during my shift, I realized my feelings were changing. I was standing at the bar while waiting for an order when Kyle walked over to the hostess stand to check the reservations. Not once did he ogle one of the other girls, but as he turned around, our eyes met, and he smiled.

That smile was for me. Just me. No one else.

I grin at my reflection in the mirror as I take the elevator up to Kyle's place. It's Monday night, which means Marilyn's is closed, and it's my one night off.

Kyle is making me dinner tonight, and I'm nervous when the doors open to the foyer. We've had some pretty heated moments, but we've never done anything more.

I'm ready to move our relationship to the next step.

"There's my gorgeous girl," Kyle says as he comes down the stairs. He walks right up to me, wraps an arm around my waist and kisses me passionately.

When he pulls back, I smile up at him. "Something smells delicious."

"I've done something different. I hope you like it," Kyle says secretively.

Taking my hand, he pulls me to the kitchen. When I see what he's done, I laugh. "We're having breakfast?"

He grins at me as he pulls out a stool for me. "Because of the hours we work, we've never had a decent breakfast before. I like the idea of starting my day with you."

Aww... he's so sweet.

We help ourselves to the various breakfast foods he has laid out on the counter. Kyle thought of everything. Eggs, bacon, hash browns, biscuits and gravy, and pancakes, damn, I'm going to roll out of here by the time we're done eating.

The conversation is light while we enjoy the feast, and I find myself smiling the entire time.

When I take my last bite, feeling like my stomach could burst, Kyle places our dirty dishes in the dishwasher. I watch as he pours us each a glass of wine.

"Let's go sit in the living room," he says, and he waits for me to get up before he follows me over to the couch.

Once I'm seated, he hands me a glass and clinks his own against mine.

"Here's to us," he whispers.

I take a sip and place the glass on the table next to me. I've never been much of a big drinker.

As I turn back, Kyle's hands frame my face, and his lips press against mine. Things heat up quickly, and soon we're breathless as we claw at each other's clothes.

I only manage to get his shirt off before he drags my jeans and panties down my legs. He pushes my shirt up and yanks my bra down, and his mouth is hot on my sensitive flesh as his lips cover a nipple.

A moan drifts from my lips as his hand slips between my legs.

Letting go of my breast, he glances up at me with a grin. "You're wet for me, gorgeous."

He quickly rolls on a condom before he covers my body and enters me.

It's been so long since I've had sex that it hurts a little. He moves faster and faster, and it makes the slight sting fade.

Claiming my mouth, he devours me. As he breaks the kiss, he thrusts deeper into me, and it hits the right spot. Pleasure ripples through me and Kyle follows right after.

Pulling out of me, Kyle's eyes lock on mine with an intense look. "I knew we would be good together. You're mine now, Evie."

I stare at the modest house with the dilapidated white picket fence, trying to imagine what it would've been like growing up here.

I picture a little girl with red pigtails, running around the yard, laughing as her daddy scoops her up and places her on his shoulders. She's on top of the world.

I finally got some information on my mother. *Josephine Bailey*. As scared as I am about what else I might learn, I know I'll always wonder if I don't go through with this.

Straightening my spine, I walk up the path. I hesitate for a second before I push through my fear and nerves, and I knock on the door.

An elderly lady opens the door, and my first thought is, could she be my grandma?

"Hi." My voice is shaky from the fear that my parents still won't want me. "I'm looking for Josephine Bailey."

The woman furrows her brow as she tries to recall the name.

"The name doesn't ring a bell. I've only lived here for four years." She stabs a thumb in the direction of the neighbor's house. "If the person you're looking for lived here before me, then Maggie will know them. Best you go ask her."

The door closes in my face before I can thank her.

I glance over at the neighboring house. It doesn't look much better. It's clear the neighborhood has fallen on hard times.

I make my way over to Maggie's house and knock. This time I'm not feeling nervous at all. Instead, I feel a sense of dread that I'll never find my parents.

A woman opens the door, and my eyes widen as I take in her appearance. Her purple hair is full of curlers, and a cigarette is dangling from her bottom lip. It looks like it's about to drop any second. A thin flannel robe covers her skinny body, and worn slippers are on her feet.

I clear my throat when she raises an eyebrow at me.

"Hi, Maggie," I say, forcing a smile to my face.

"Do I know you?" she says, her voice gruff from years of smoking. She squints her eyes and looks at me as if she's seen me before but can't quite place where.

"Uhm… no. I'm looking for Josephine Bailey. I was wondering if you knew her?"

Her mouth gapes open, and the cigarette falls to the floor. Slapping her hand over her heart, her eyes grow wide as saucers.

"Can it be?" With trembling fingers, she grabs the glasses hanging around her neck and shoves them onto her nose. "As I live and breathe," she whispers. "I thought he'd thrown you in the river."

Confused and shocked by her words, I can only stare at her.

She reaches a wrinkly hand out to me, and her eyes are filled with disbelief as she touches my cheeks.

"My God, you're the spitting image of Joey," she breathes.

The next second she grabs hold of my arm and yanks me into the house. Keeping hold of me, she continues to stare at me for a long while.

I swallow hard and ask the one question I fear most, "Did you know my mom?"

She starts to nod her head as her face fills with sadness, and it makes my heart sink into the floorboards beneath my feet.

"Let's have some tea."

I follow her to the kitchen and hardly take in the worn state of everything inside the house. I just want to know what happened to my mom and dad. Even if they died, it would be more than I have now. At least, I'll know they didn't leave me by choice, and that makes all the difference.

I sit down on a rickety chair and wait for Maggie to finish making the tea.

When she places a cracked cup in front of me, I smile gratefully.

"Thank you. Can you tell me more about my mom?" I ask,, hopefully.

Maggie lights a cigarette before her tired brown eyes lock on mine.

"It's a sad story. What happened to those kids, it's this town's biggest tragedy."

I grip my hands together on my lap, steeling myself as best I can for what's to come.

"What did you say your name was?" Maggie asks as a ball of smoke billows around her head.

"Evie Cole," I whisper.

Maggie starts to blink rapidly as she gets emotional.

"At least you got your daddy's last name. That's good," she says, nodding to herself.

"Hayden Cole?" I ask to make sure I have the right name.

"Yeah, Hayden Dean Cole and Josephine Bailey. You should know your parents loved each other very much."

I lick my dry lips and ask, "What happened to them?"

Maggie takes one last deep drag before she kills the cigarette in an overfull ashtray.

"I still have some of Joey's things. I didn't have the heart to throw them out."

As she gets up and shuffles out of the room, I bite my bottom lip, and my right leg starts to jump. It doesn't take Maggie long to come back with a shoebox. Besides the coloring of age, the box is in better shape than anything else I've seen in this town.

"Joe Bailey was slapped upside the head by the devil himself. He's your granddaddy. He had a mean streak, and the drinking only made it worse. Your grandmamma died giving birth to your mamma, just like your mamma died giving birth to you."

Sorrow for a woman I've never known floods my heart. My eyes begin to burn, and I fight hard to keep the tears back.

Maggie opens the box, taking a faded photo from it. She hands it to me, and when I see the young couple smiling up at the camera from where they're sitting at this very table, my sight blurs.

I blink quickly, wanting to take in everything about them. The girl is pretty, and her smile is so broad, it doesn't look like she has a care in the world. She has the same wild red hair as me. We could've been twins. My eyes skip to my dad's face.

"You got your daddy's eyes. Every girl in town was crazy for that boy."

A tear escapes my eye, and I wipe it away with the back of my hand.

"But he loved my mom," I whisper, carefully caressing my thumb over their faces. This is the closest I'll ever get to touching them.

"After the funeral, I asked Joe what happened to you. He never answered me. He took the secret to his grave a week after Joey died. Drowned himself in one too many bottles of brandy."

"How old was my mom when she gave birth to me?" I have so many questions about my parents, but that's the first one that comes to mind.

"She was eighteen. Joey and Hayden were high school sweethearts. Hayden made an honest woman of your mamma. They got engaged before he left to serve his time for his country."

Another tear rolls down my cheek, but this time I leave it as I whisper, "Did he die while serving?"

"Hayden was an only child. His mamma," she pauses to light a cigarette, "your grandmamma died

213

during his senior year. That boy worked his fingers to the bone so he could finish school. He had so much potential. We all thought Hayden and Joey would make it out of this town and have themselves a fairytale life in the city."

Maggie finishes her tea before she digs into the box again. She takes out a stack of the letters, tied neatly with a pale pink ribbon.

"These were the letters your daddy wrote while he was serving. I couldn't find any from after your momma died. I tried writing to the address on the back, to give Hayden my condolences, but I never received anything in return."

"Did he come back here after his tour was up?"

Maggie shrugs, and it makes my heart start to thump in my chest.

"No one knows what happened to Hayden. I assumed he died. He never came back here."

A tiny seed of hope pushes through my sorrow. "He could still be alive?"

Maggie lets out a huff of air. "Hayden lived for Joey. If he did survive the army, it would be so sad knowing he had to continue living without her."

Maggie takes a plain silver band from the box.

214

"This was your mamma's ring." With trembling fingers, I take it from Maggie. She leans closer to me. "Put it on. Let's see if it fits."

My chest fills to the brim with emotions as I slip the ring onto my left hand. It's a little too big, so I switch it over to my right hand.

A satisfied smile settles on Maggie's wrinkled face.

"You should wear it. Joey and Hayden would've wanted it that way."

I visit with Maggie for a couple of hours, listening to stories of my parents and their love before I get up to leave.

"Thank you so much for agreeing to see me, and thank you for keeping my mom's things safe all these years."

"You're welcome, Evie." Her eyes glide over me, and she smiles proudly. "You know, it's comforting to know that their love survived the tragedy."

I frown, not understanding what she means.

"It's you, child. You are the living proof of Hayden and Joey's love. It gives my old heart some peace."

I hug Maggie and giving her one last smile. I walk away richer than when I got here. I have a photo of my parents, the letters from Dad, and Mom's ring.

But the most important thing is that they never left me.

Chapter 26

Rhett

Getting out of the shower, I throw on a shirt and jeans, along with my boots, before grabbing my car keys and phone.

It's become a routine to spend my Saturday nights at *Senses*. It's an exclusive club where you pay an arm, leg, and half a kidney to get in. The expensive entrance ticket keeps the trash out.

Driving to the club, my mind returns to Evie for the umpteenth time. I don't know how to approach her. I've thought of everything from just showing up at her apartment, to hiring a fucking band to serenade her. I chuckle at the last idea, thinking that might be a bit overkill.

Parking my car, I get out and walk to the entrance. The bouncer, who isn't much bigger than me, pats me down before I'm allowed to enter. I pay the five-hundred-dollar entrance fee, then walk through to the changing room. I strip out of my clothes, and like always, I keep my boxers on.

I pull the mask onto my face, covering the area around my eyes. The mask doesn't hide much of your face. It allows people to live the fantasy of fucking a stranger and not having to worry you'll recognize them the next week in a meeting.

Some of the people coming here choose to go in butt naked, but most of us keep something on.

Walking into the central dance area, I scan the dimly lit room before making my way over to the huge bar.

"Macallan," I say to the bartender when he looks at me.

He nods subtly and takes care as he pours two ounces over a single round ice cube in a crystal tumbler.

He gently slides it over to me. "Your charity of choice, Sir?"

The sixty-four-thousand-dollars they charge for the single malt gets donated to a charity of my choice. It's really a win-win for me.

"Summer's Forever Foundation," I say as I hand over my card.

After the fee is charged, I take my whiskey and walk over to one of the many couches they have positioned around the dance floor.

I take a seat and savor my drink while I look at the people dancing.

When I started coming here, I used to get excited. I'd fuck the first girl I laid eyes on. But the excitement is long gone. Now I sit and wait for the girl to come to me. I let her fuck me while I finish my drink, then I leave.

The only reason I still come here is that it's a safe place to get laid. I have no desire to go from bar to bar, or club to club, hoping to find a woman decent enough to use for a one-night stand.

It's convenient this way. Both parties know what they're getting, and it doesn't include any form of commitment.

My drink is almost finished when a dark-haired woman saunters over to me. I let my eyes glide over her toned body. Lifting my hand, I indicate for her to twirl in a circle for me. With the seductive beat filling the air, I never try to talk to anyone. I don't come here to make conversation anyway.

The dark-haired beauty turns slowly, displaying all her assets. I've had worse, so with a lift of my chin, I give her the club sign that I accept her offer.

The corner of her mouth lifts slightly as she closes the distance between us.

Her eyes drop to my boxers, and she lifts an eyebrow. Knowing what she wants, I only shove my boxers down enough to free my cock.

Her tongue darts out, and she licks her lips as she takes a condom from the stand next to the couch. That's another added bonus. The club supplies an endless amount of condoms.

She rips the foil and removing the rubber, she bends at the waist, letting her tits hang right in front of my line of sight, as she rolls the condom onto my cock.

She's an experienced member. Good. At least the fuck will be worth my time.

Straightening back up, she walks over to the display case and picks a pair of ankle and wrist cuff restraints. When she returns, she offers the black velvet restraints to me. I take them from her and wait for her to turn around until she's facing the dance floor. I crouch down in front of her and position a cuff around each of her ankles. She bends at the waist, giving me access to her wrists, and I secure the cuffs.

Because I'm not a total asshole – yet – I glance up at her and brushing my knuckles over her cheek, I lean forward and press a soft kiss to the corner of her mouth.

Getting up, I place my right hand on the back of her neck and trailing my fingers down her spine, I walk back to the couch and sit down. With her ass at my eye level, I bring my finger down the crack of her ass.

Circling her clit, I can feel that she's already wet. At least we won't need lube. I push a finger inside her pussy and work her slowly.

One of the primary rules of the club is that both parties have to be satisfied. I suppose it's their way of keeping their clients happy.

With my middle finger working her pussy, I rub my thumb over her ass, every now and then stretching her a bit. She presses her ass into my hand and grinds, and I can feel her pussy gripping me with excitement.

Thank fuck, she likes it dirty like me.

I stand up, and not bothering to shove my boxers any lower, I take hold of my cock and position it at her ass. Moving my right arm around the front of her, I drive two fingers back into her pussy. I force the head of my cock inside her ass, and after the initial resistance, the rest of me slips in with ease. A shudder ripples through her as I pull back a little.

I keep my pace slow at first, but soon I'm pumping into her hard and fast. Needing for her to orgasm, I pinch her clit hard. Her ass shudders against me as she finally comes, and it doesn't take long for me to follow.

As soon as I'm done, I pull out of her. I grab paper towels from the table containing the condoms and clean myself. I take a second to shove my cock back into my boxers before I help her out of the cuffs.

When she straightens up, there's a satisfied smile on her face. She mouths the words 'thank you' and saunters away from me.

Picking up the tumbler, I take the last sip of whiskey before I place the restraints back on the display case.

That's me for tonight.

I walk back to the changing room, and first, wash my hands a couple of times before I get dressed.

Once I'm back home and taking a quick shower, my thoughts return to Evie, and for the first time, I feel guilty that the woman I fucked isn't the woman I love.

Chapter 27

Evie

I've been searching for my dad. Finding out what happened to him has become my primary focus.

I contacted the base he was stationed at when I was born, and after a painfully long search, it looks like I might have found someone who will be able to tell me what happened to my dad.

I'm at MacArthur Park, standing by the lake where we agreed to meet. Glancing at my watch, my stomach tightens with nerves. He'll be here any second now.

When John Adams first responded to one of the dozens of emails I sent out, I wasn't very hopeful. He asked some questions about me and then said he'd be in touch.

It took him two weeks to get back to me. He said he wanted to meet in person, that he had answers for some of my questions.

I hope he does. I stare at the water, wondering what answers he has for me. I've given up staring at every face passing me by. I should have asked him what he looks like. It was stupid of me not to.

"Evie." My name is so soft, and I almost think I imagined it.

I glance over my shoulder and seeing a man standing a few feet from me, I turn around.

He takes a step back as his eyes widen with shock. It looks like he's seen a ghost.

"Are you John?" I ask, an anxious smile wavering on my lips.

He shakes his head, and although his lips part, he doesn't speak for another minute.

"I'm Hayden Cole," he says, his voice hoarse.

My eyes widen as the name sinks in. My breaths speed up, and no matter how hard I fight to keep control of the emotions barreling through me, tears fill my eyes.

"You're Hayden Cole? Josephine Bailey's fiancé?" I ask to make sure.

My eyes flit over him, trying to match him to the young man in the photo. My hand is trembling so badly, I almost drop the photo as I take it from my bag. I look at the face of my father on the photo, then back to the man.

They both have green eyes. *My eyes.*

They both have dark brown hair.

The photo shows a scar through his left eyebrow.

I look up, and my breath catches when I see the scar.

He takes a shuddering breath, and when the first tear rolls down his cheek, he says, "I was told you didn't make it. I looked for you. I went to the hospital and was told my daughter died."

I shake my head and whisper, "I didn't."

We just stare at each other, and it feels like time is standing still.

Slowly, he lifts his hand and cups my cheek. Brushing his thumb over the swell of my cheek, his tears begin to fall faster. My eyes are on fire, and my throat is stuffed full of emotions.

"My God. You're alive," he whispers, his voice cracking over the words.

He takes a step forward, and his arms wrap around me. The moment I bury my face in his chest, it feels like I shatter. If he lets go of me now, my pieces will just crumble to the floor.

A cry forces its way through my throat, and I press harder into my father's chest so I can smother the sound.

He holds me so close, his body jerking from his own cries, as he starts to place kisses along the side of my head.

He pulls slightly back, framing my face with both his hands. His eyes hold mine, and I see the sorrow of lost time, but I also see the happiness of now, and the hope of a future together.

"I saw your death certificate, Evie. I didn't stop until I saw on paper that you were dead. But even afterward, I always had this feeling that you didn't die. I thought you were my guardian angel watching over me."

"I thought you didn't want me," I whisper.

He pulls me to his chest again, as he says, "I wanted you with every fiber of my being. Not a day has passed, I didn't think of you and your mom. No matter where I was, you were both there with me."

We hold each other until I've lost all track of time.

Dad pulls back, and taking my hand, he pulls me over to a nearby bench. Once seated, he turns his body to face me and holds my hand in both of his.

A smile begins to warm his face as his eyes keep darting over my face.

"You're just as beautiful as your mother. When you turned around, I thought my mind was playing tricks on me."

I swallow and straightening my spine, I say, "I met Maggie. She was Mom's neighbor. She told me what she could, and she gave me some stuff."

I hold out my right hand so he can see the ring. I haven't taken it off since I put it on.

"That's your mother's ring," he says, his voice filled with a mixture of amazement and grief.

"I hope it's okay that I wear it?" I half ask, half say, not sure how he'll feel about it.

He nods. "It's more than okay. She would've wanted that."

When it started to grow dark, Dad suggested we go for dinner. While we walked to the restaurant, I quickly texted Kyle to let him know I wouldn't be coming in to work tonight.

Once we've placed our orders, Dad reaches across the table and holds my hand. It's like he's scared to let go of me for even a minute.

"Are you married?" I ask. I'm a little terrified he might have a family, and they won't accept me.

He shakes his head, giving my hand a squeeze. "After I lost your mother and you… thought that I lost you… I just worked."

"Are you still in the military?"

I have so many questions. I wish I could ask them all at once, so I don't forget any of them.

"I actually never joined the military. I joined the navy."

"Oh," I say, feeling dumb. I don't know much about how it works. To me, the military is the military.

His eyes settle on mine, and it feels like he's trying to look inside my heart.

"I'm a Navy SEAL." He chuckles and shakes his head. "Not that I've been a good one, seeing as I didn't find you."

"You didn't know," I whisper, hating what happened to us, but not wanting him to take the blame.

A muscle starts to tick in his jaw, and a wave of anger washes over his face. It's quick before he regains control over his emotions.

"I'm going to find out what happened. Someone is going to pay for taking you from me." His words are filled with so much determination, it sends a shiver racing down my spine.

The waitress brings our food, and once she's gone, Dad says, "You didn't give up."

I'm so surprised by the proud look on his face that I just sit there blinking. No one has ever looked at me like that.

He smiles, and it warms his eyes. "Your mom wouldn't have given up either."

Chapter 28

Rhett

"You rang, oh hunky one of mine?" Miss Sebastian says as she walks into my office.

My head snaps up from where I was focusing on a spreadsheet.

"I messaged you a minute ago," I say. "How did you get here so fast?"

"As always, my timing is perfect... aaaand I had lunch with the girls, so we decided to bring over some food for our men."

Hearing the word food, my eyes dart to her hands. "Where's mine?"

Miss Sebastian rolls her eyes as she places a paper bag on my desk. "You'd swear I never feed you," she mumbles while making herself comfortable in a chair across from me.

Usually, I'd be tearing at the bag to get to the food, but not today.

Miss Sebastian notices the serious look on my face, which makes her manicured eyebrows dart into her hairline. "Hold that thought," she says.

Getting up, she closes the office door and locks it. Her ass hardly touches the chair before she shoots up again, reaches over my desk to unplug the desk phone. Then she proceeds to switch off my cell and her own before she finally slumps back in the chair.

"Now we won't be disturbed. What's wrong?"

I've never seen her so serious before. It's actually a little scary.

"Uhm... well... you see –"

Her eyebrows draw together as she leans across the desk, placing her hand on mine.

"You're a hot mess, my babykins! Who do I need to kill? Just give me the name, and I'll take care of them. No one will be able to trace it back to you by the time I'm done."

I start to laugh, but at the same time, my heart overflows with love for this woman. Since I've met her, she's shot up the ranks to the number one spot in my heart.

"You don't have to kill anyone," I say, giving her a grateful smile. "I need... ahh..." I pinch my eyes

231

closed, hoping I won't regret this. "I need your help with a woman."

"Ahhhhhhhhhhhhhhhhhhhhhhhh!"

Fuck, my ears are going to bleed.

"OhmyGodI'mgonnadie."

Oh shit.

"Mychunkofhunkfinallyfoundawoman."

Here we go.

I sit back as Miss Sebastian fires the questions at me one after the other.

"Who is she?"

"Do I know her?"

"What's her name?"

Her words run together as she's overtaken with excitement, and I'm already regretting asking her.

Silence fills the office as she sits and bounces on her chair, with a smile so broad I swear if she didn't have ears, it would wrap right around her head.

"It's Evie Cole. I —"

"AhhhhhhhohmyGodIknewyoustilllovedher!"

I slump back in my chair and close my eyes.

Yep, this was a huge mistake.

"Don't roll your eyes at me! I can see them moving even if you close them," Miss Sebastian snaps at me.

I start to laugh because nothing escapes her attention. When I look at her, the smile is still plastered all over her face.

"What do you need me to do?"

Finally, we get to the reason I sent her a message, asking if I could come over for coffee after work.

"I fucked up."

I've never seen a smile vanish so fast before.

"What did you do?" Miss Sebastian pulls a face as if I'm about to throw shit at her.

"I didn't trust Evie." Confusion makes her eyes blink rapidly, so I quickly give her the short version. "I have some issues I'm dealing with. I don't trust easily."

Miss Sebastian's eyebrows pop up again, and I let out a heavy sigh.

"Of course, I trust you. You know, it's very distracting having a conversation with your facial expressions."

"You trust me with your little black heart. It's all that matters. Carry on. You didn't trust Evie because, like my other chunk of hunks, you were too wrapped up in your asshole-ish selves to see a good thing when it was slapping y'all right in the face."

"That about sums it up. Good, we're on the same page. I don't know how to worm myself back into Evie's life."

"Babykins, I've seen your ding-dong when you had that godawful stomach bug. In my professional opinion, which counts for a hell of a lot, seeing as I see a fair amount of ding dongs on a daily basis, your ding-dong cannot be compared to a worm."

She sucks in a breath of air after getting all of that out.

"Miss Sebastian, can you try and focus? We're not talking about dicks now. We're talking about me finding a way to get back into Evie's life."

"Well, that's easy-peasy. Just pick up the damn phone and talk to the woman." She gives me an incredulous look as if she can't believe I haven't thought of something so simple.

"I need to do something bigger than a call. Something that says I'm sorry for being a bastard."

Miss Sebastian thinks about it for a while.

"My babykins," she says, giving me a look filled with pity, "I'm afraid you only have two choices. You either call the woman, or you go see her in person. I, personally, would prefer you see her face to face. Doing anything else at this point will be a waste of your time, and honestly, plain creepy. You're going to have to start slow and work your way back into her good graces the old-fashion way."

I let out a heavy sigh. I'm scared to death that the second Evie hears my voice, she makes a run for it.

Miss Sebastian switches on her phone, and I watch her type something. It gives me time to think about what she just said. Do I call Evie, or do I just show up at her place?

Miss Sebastian suddenly smiles triumphantly. The next second she puts the phone to her ear.

"Hi, Evie?" Her smile widens as my heart stops. "This is Miss Sebastian. I'm a friend of... oh, Willow mentioned me. That's wonderful. Was it all good things?"

My mouth opens, but only a strangled sound comes out.

"Aww... that's so sweet of my angel-girl. Anyhow, I'm also a close friend of Rhett Daniels. Oh, but not so close that we bow-chika-wow-wow. I'm happily married. But then, if I weren't, I'd definitely consider it. You've seen the man. He's seriously fine-looking."

"WHAT THE FUCK," I mouth the words at her. I can't believe she just said that to Evie.

"Moving along, from what I understand, his assholishness far outweighed his sexiness, and he owes you an apology. Would you mind meeting with him?"

Miss Sebastian glances down at her nails, frowns, and then takes a closer look at her hands.

"Ah-ha."

"Mmmm."

"Oh."

"Ugh."

What the hell was the ugh for? I lean down, my head almost touching the desk as I try to catch her eyes.

"I agree with you, girl."

She starts to nod.

"I don't blame you."

I dart up and reach over the desk, grabbing the phone from Miss Sebastian.

I put the phone to my ear. "Evie?"

There's total silence on the other side of the call. I look at the screen, and when I see that there is no call, I don't know if I should hug Miss Sebastian or strangle her bedazzled ass.

Miss Sebastian stands up, takes her phone back, and shoves it in her bag. She looks at me with the sweetest smile, and cheerfully says, "Either you call Evie now, or the conversation you just heard will be happening for real."

She places her hand on my arm, and standing on her toes, she presses a kiss to my cheek.

"I love you, Rhett. I want to see you find your own happiness. I've gotten Evie's number and address from Willow, and I've forwarded it to you. Talk to Evie. Delaying it further won't make it any better."

I wrap my arms around her and press a kiss to the top of her head.

"You're scary when you're serious," I whisper.

She pulls back and places her hand on my chest, and I cover hers with mine, giving it a squeeze.

"I'm only serious when it comes to someone I love, and you, my babykins, have always had a special place in my heart."

I give her another hug before she leaves.

Chapter 29

Evie

I drop the spoon and dive for my phone as it starts to ring, thinking it's Dad, and he's calling to cancel our dinner plans.

"Hi," I say, sounding a little out of breath.

"Hey, gorgeous," Kyle says.

Hearing Kyle's voice instead, I quickly turn back to the stove and continue to stir the pasta sauce.

"Oh, hey." I stir a little faster so it won't make clots as it thickens.

"Who's there?" he asks sharply.

"No one. I'm making dinner. You caught me making a sauce."

"Don't fucking lie to me, Evie!" He shouts, scaring me, and I almost drop the phone.

I'm shocked out of my mind that Kyle just shouted at me. He's never spoken to me like that. Sure we've had our moments over the past month because I haven't been spending as much time with him as I used to, but I thought he understood that it was important to me to spend time with my dad.

"Who the fuck is there? Are you fucking someone else? I swear if I catch you with another –"

"No one is here, Kyle," I say. "I'm making dinner for my dad. He's coming over. I told you this when we spoke earlier."

"You fucking bitch. I knew it. You tell whoever's there, that you're mine," he hisses.

Before I can think of something to reply, he cuts the call, leaving me staring at the ruined sauce.

I remove the pot from the stove and start the whole process over while my mind reels.

What just happened?

That couldn't have been Kyle. He's always sweet and gentle with me.

I manage to make the sauce without it ruining, and when everything is ready, I go sit on the couch and stare blankly at the floor.

How could I have been so wrong about Kyle?

A knock on my door pulls me out of my confused thoughts, and I get up. Opening the door, I smile when I see Dad.

"You made it," I say as I move forward to hug him.

We've spent almost every day together since we found each other a month ago. With Dad still working as an active Navy SEAL, we're making the most of our time together before he gets sent away.

Hugging me tightly, he presses a kiss to the top of my head.

"What smells so good?" he asks while we walk into the living room.

"The other day you mentioned you loved pasta, so I made some for dinner."

A broad smile spreads across his face, and it feels so good to know I'm responsible for it.

"If it's half as good as your mom's, I'll have to spend an extra hour at the gym tomorrow."

I prepare two plates for us and hand Dad his as we sit down on the couch.

I'm just about to apologize that I don't have a table we can sit at, when Dad says, "I know it's soon, but I want you to think about moving into my apartment. I'm away often, and the place just stands empty."

My lips part and I can't make the words come out.

A sad look makes me keep quiet, as he continues, "I didn't have a chance to raise you, Evie. I missed out on so many important parts of your life. I'd like a chance to make up for that. I'd like a chance to be your father. I want to take care of my little girl. I can't let you live here. It's not safe. I worry every time I have to leave you here."

"Daddy," I whisper as I place my hand on his arm. When he watches me with so much intensity, as if my following words might either make or break him, I smile. "Of course, I will. That way, I can make sure you eat a decent meal every day."

Surprise flashes over his face. "You will? Did you just agree to let me take care of you?"

I nod and begin to laugh. "Yes, Dad." My laughter fades away, and my bottom lip starts to tremble as I say, "Mostly, I want to be a family. You don't have to take care of me. I just want to feel what it's like to have a family home."

He moves our plates so fast to the coffee table and wraps me in his arms, that a breath rushes from me.

"I'm going to give you all of that and so much more. I'm going to make it up to you, Evie. I promise."

I nod as I curl deeper into his embrace. I close my eyes, and for the millionth time, I send up a prayer of thanks that I found my dad.

We pick up our plates and take a couple of bites. I observe Dad's face to see if he likes it.

As he chews, his eyes slowly drift close, and a look of pure appreciation fills his face. He swallows, and a moment later, when he opens his eyes, they're shining with tears. "It tastes exactly the same as your mom's." Then he teases, "I'm so damn grateful you don't cook like me. I burn everything in sight."

When we've finished our meals, I make us some coffee.

After sitting down again, Dad asks, "Can we go to a mall tomorrow? I want to see what kind of things you like."

I let out a little burst of laughter. "I'm not a huge fan of shopping."

"Not?" The surprise on his face is quite funny. "Your mom loved to shop. What do you like to do?"

"There is one thing I've always wanted to do," I say, biting my bottom lip.

"What's that?"

"Jump out of a plane."

His mouth drops open. It seems I've just shocked my dad.

Then he grins at me, looking all proud.

"Finally, you got something from me besides your eyes."

My eyes widen with excitement. "Does that mean you'll take me?"

"As long as you're strapped to me, we can jump out of planes as many times as you want."

I let out a shriek of joy as I throw my arms around his neck. "And can we go paragliding, and bungee jumping, and rappelling, and –"

My words are cut off when Dad starts to laugh.

"We can do all those things."

What was I thinking?

I can't do this.

I try to take a step away from the edge, but being strapped to Dad's chest stops me.

Oh crap.

I'm doing this.

Dad moves forward, and we start to tip forward. I let out a scream that's slammed right back into my throat as the air hits me in the face.

A lifetime passes where I can only feel my heart racing madly in my chest. My body is suddenly jerked upwards, and then it feels like a bubble of calm wraps around me.

Dad points to something on the ground, and I look down.

Oh wow. Everything is so small. I see patches of land, buildings, trees, and looking to my left, I see the ocean.

As Dad steers us towards the ground, I close my eyes and allow myself to feel this moment. It's just my father and me, and we're on top of the world.

Nearing the ground, I pull my legs up like Dad told me to, and he takes the brunt of the impact. I expected us to roll across the grass, but instead, Dad takes a few steps before bringing us to a stop.

His hands move so fast, I can't keep track of everything he's doing, and before I know it, we're unclasped, and he's turning me around. His eyes search my face, and when I grin, he relaxes visibly.

"That was amazing," I yell.

I throw myself at him, not even thinking that I might knock him off balance. He catches me against his solid chest. I wrap my arms tighter around his neck and bury my face in his shoulder, as my emotions sky-rocket.

"I'm so glad I found you," I cry. "I've only had you a few weeks, and already I can't imagine my life without you."

"You'll never have to, Evie. I'm here now, and I'm never leaving you."

Hearing the promise in his words fills me with a sense of belonging and safety. It's like a security blanket has been wrapped around my heart.

When Dad sets me down on my feet, I look up into his eyes.

"How did I get so lucky?" I whisper. "You're everything I dreamt a father would be."

"It's only because I had twenty-six years of dreaming what it would be like to have you in my life."

Chapter 30

Rhett

I lift my hand to knock on the door but freeze before I can go through with it. I can't remember a time in my life where I've been so nervous. Hell, not even when I lost my virginity.

I've come this far, and I'm not about to back out.

"You've got this," I whisper to myself as I knock on the door.

I hear movement on the other side of the door, and as it opens, Evie says, "You're early."

For a second, she looks so happy, and her eyes sparkle. I drink in everything about her in a split-second. Her hair is longer. There's a glow to her I've never seen before.

But fuck, she's even more beautiful than I remember.

Then her face freezes and the joy fades away, the light in her eyes dim, and I know it's all because I'm standing in front of her.

"Hi, Evie," I whisper. When she takes a step backward, I dart forward and place my hand on the door so she can't slam it in my face. "Just give me five minutes."

She looks visibly shaken from seeing me, and I hate that I've fucked-up so badly.

She steps to the side and whispers, "Come in."

That's a good sign, right?

She doesn't close the door behind me but instead leaves it wide open.

My eyes dart around her home. I smile when I see Evie's things everywhere.

"I know it's been years," I say as I bring my eyes back to her, "and that we didn't part on the best of terms, but I'd like to explain myself."

"You don't have to," she says. "You don't owe me anything."

"I do, Evie. I owe you an apology."

She furrows her brow. "For what?"

"You can do it," I tell myself silently. *"Be honest with her."*

"For not believing in you," I say. I clear my throat, and then I get it all off my chest. "For not trusting you when you never gave me any reason not to. For being stubborn. For being self-absorbed. For not loving you the way you deserve to be loved when I had the chance. Mostly, I'm sorry for letting you go. I'm sorry it took me six years to realize what I have lost."

She wraps her arms around herself. "It's okay. It's been six years."

Things are taking a turn for the awkward, so I quickly ask, "How have you been?"

A small smile tugs at her lips. "Actually, things have never been better."

Dreading the answer, I ask it anyway, "Have you met someone?"

She chuckles, but it's a sharp sound. "Does it matter? Why are you doing this, Rhett? You've been in LA for over a year. Why reach out to me now?"

"Because I was scared out of my mind." The brutally honest words leave my mouth before I'm even done thinking them. "I have thought of you every day since you left. Watching you drive away, it ripped my heart out. I kept pushing you away because I wanted to save myself from that kind of pain, but in the end, it happened anyway."

"I'm sorry," she whispers.

"I might not get this opportunity again, so here goes nothing. I don't trust easily. You know that,right?"

Shit, I'm messing this up.

I suck in a deep breath and try again, "After my parents died, none of our family wanted to take care of Mia and me. If it weren't for Mr. Hayes, we could've ended up being separated, or worse. The second they found out the wealthy Christopher Hayes was taking care of us, they were all suddenly very willing to take us in. For a price, of course. That was my first lesson on how people only saw dollar signs when they looked at me."

I can see my words are getting through to Evie, so I continue, "I never knew whether someone really cared about me, or whether they were only interested in what they could get from me. Besides that, no one ever stuck around. My parents died. Jaxon and Logan's dad ran off with Carter's mother. Marcus' dad killed his mom and sister. My entire life, people were hurting each other. Girls only wanted to be with me because I was good for their social status. I could never trust anyone."

Evie stares at me for a while before she whispers, "I wish you had told me all of this before I left."

"I was a coward, Evie. It was easier to hide behind my bullshit jokes and hardass mask."

I can't take my eyes off of her as I watch her process everything I just said. And it sucks that my time with her is almost up. Whoever Evie's waiting for will be here at any moment.

I place my business card on her coffee table. "I'd like to have coffee with you, Evie. It would be nice to catch up."

She nods and draws her bottom lip in between her teeth as she glances at my card.

"I miss you," I whisper.

She smiles sadly, and I'm surprised when she admits, "I've missed you too."

"When you're ready to have coffee with me, please call or text. Hell, you can send a smoke signal."

She lets out a little burst of laughter. Fuck, I've missed that sound so much.

I walk to the door and turn back one last time. "You look happy, Evie. I'm glad. No one deserves it more than you."

"Thank you, Rhett. I'll be in touch."

Taking one last look at her, I turn around to leave, but instead, I come face to face with the scariest looking man I've ever laid eyes on.

I can hold my own in a fight, but my gut tells me that few have gone up against this guy, and survived to tell the tale.

"Hi," he says, reaching a hand out to me. "I'm Hayden Cole. Who are you?"

Holy fuck. He's intense.

I take his hand and say, "Rhett Daniels."

Evie pops up next to us, and the huge smile I saw when she opened the door is back on her face. She stands on her toes, and I watch as the man leans a little down so Evie can reach his cheek where she plants a firm kiss.

She takes hold of his arm and pulls his hand out of mine, then locks it in a tight grip to her chest.

"Morning, Daddy," she says, and the two words send ripples of shock through my entire body.

"Daddy?" I echo her like an idiot.

Hayden's eyes snap back to mine, and I quickly explain, "Sorry, the last time Evie and I spoke, she didn't know who her parents were."

251

"How do you and Rhett know each other?" he asks Evie, but he never takes his eyes off me.

Shit, I have never been so intimidated by a girl's father before.

Evie clears her throat, and her cheeks flush pink as she says, "He's the guy I told you about. Rhett helped me get off the street."

Hayden's facial expression changes so fast, I actually blink to make sure I'm not imagining things. It's as if he just threw an off switch. Gone is the Hulk, and he's back to being Bruce Banner.

"Thank you," he says, as he pulls his arm free from Evie's death grip, and holds his hand out to me once more. I shake his hand, and this time he doesn't try to break any bones. "Thank you for taking care of my daughter when I couldn't."

I have a million questions, but now is definitely not the right time to ask them. I nod because saying something as stupid as *you're welcome* or *it's a pleasure*, doesn't sound right.

My manners haven't entirely up and left me. "It was nice meeting you, Sir."

I smile at Evie. "Talk to you soon."

Not waiting for them to reply, I walk away.

Fuck, that was unexpected. Evie found her dad. I wonder what else has changed in her life.

Chapter 31

Evie

When I saw Rhett standing in front of me, I couldn't believe my eyes. It's been so long since I last saw him, but at that moment, it felt like the past six years were nothing but a wrinkle in time.

I was overwhelmed by everything he told me, especially after the shock I had from seeing him.

I texted Rhett yesterday and asked him to meet me at the same park where I met Dad. I'm hoping for the same outcome between Rhett and me, that I had with Dad.

With my hands tucked deep in the pockets of my coat, I walk into the park. As I near the lake, I see Rhett waiting for me. It's an odd twist of fate. This time Rhett is the lost one, and I'm the one who thought what we shared had died.

"Rhett," I whisper from behind him. He swings around, and our eyes lock.

"You came," he says, sounding relieved.

"I did. I thought about what you said," I say. "I don't want you to feel bad about what happened. We were so young. Young and stupid. We thought we knew everything, and it turned out we understood nothing."

I feel so sad as I whisper the next words, but they are true, and I can't ignore them. "We understood nothing about each other. I fell in love with the guy who saved me. It was so easy. But I never really knew the real you."

Rhett glances to the side, and I hate that my words are hurting him.

"I understand," he whispers.

"Do you? You have a tendency to jump to conclusions," I say when I see the resigned look on his face.

"I thought you didn't know me?" he can't help but tease.

"Not as well as you should know someone you claim to love."

"Claim to love?" he asks, and seeing the hope creep back into his eyes, I know I made the right decision.

"I'd like to catch up, Rhett. I'd like to hear about the past six years. I meant it when I said I missed you. You were the first important person in my life. Because of you, I searched for my parents. Every important decision I've made is in some way connected to you. We were good friends, and at the very least, I'd like for us to get back to that."

Rhett closes his eyes, and relief relaxes his features. In some ways, he still looks like my Rhett, but in many ways, he's become a man... a stranger.

His jaw is more pronounced, and there's no sign of the boyish features I fell in love with.

When he opens his eyes, he holds out his hand to me. "No more bullshit. No secrets. I'd love it so fucking much to be your friend again."

I place my hand in his, and we shake as I whisper, "It's a deal."

Rhett chuckles and suddenly yanks me forward. When I crash into his chest, his arms wrap around me.

He holds me tight and whispers, "I'm sorry I broke my promise to you, Evie. The love I felt for you scared me so much."

I nod against his chest. "The love I felt for you scared me too."

He lets go of me so fast, I almost lose my balance.

"Wait here," he says, and then I watch as he jogs away from me. He disappears behind some trees, leaving me to wonder what he's up to.

"Excuse me," he suddenly says behind me.

I swing around, wondering how he got behind me without me noticing.

Before I can ask, he says, "I was wondering if you've seen my jaw because I dropped it when I saw you."

The pick-up line is so lame that I burst out laughing.

He holds his hand out to me again. "I'm Rhett Daniels."

Finally catching on to what he's doing, I place my hand in his. "Evie Cole."

"It's nice to meet you, Evie."

"Likewise," I whisper.

"Can I take you for coffee?" he asks, a playful grin lighting up his dark eyes.

"I'd like that."

We walk to the nearest Starbucks, and I grab us a table, while Rhett places our order.

When we're both settled with a steaming beverage in our hands, I ask, "What's your biggest fear?"

"There's the Evie, I remember. Not scared to ask deep questions," he teases, but then his eyes get serious. "My biggest fear is not living up to the man, my goddaughter thinks I am."

"Willow has tried to keep me up to date with everything that's been happening. I know most of the guys have children now, but which one is your goddaughter?"

"Danny." Just saying her name makes a love I've never seen before shine from Rhett's eyes. "She's Carter and Della's oldest."

"I hope I'll get to meet her one day," I say, meaning every word.

Rhett chuckles, and for a moment, he looks a little embarrassed as he says, "She can't wait to meet you. A few months back, we were watching Frozen, and she asked me when I'll find my Elsa." Rhett pauses, then asks, "Have you watched Frozen?"

I laugh, "Yeah, but if you tell anyone, I'll deny it."

He chuckles, and continues, "I told Danny that I've already met my Anna, but she was having an adventure."

It takes a minute for me to grasp what Rhett just said.

"I'm your Anna?"

"Yeah, pretty much from the first moment I laid eyes on you."

It's going to take me a while to get used to this side of Rhett. I remember him being guarded, and having him be so open with me is a little mind-blowing.

"What's your biggest fear?" Rhett asks.

Now that Dad is in my life, it's no longer being alone.

"I'm scared," I pause, hating to even say the words out loud. "I'm scared, my dad will leave for work, and he won't come back."

Rhett reaches across the table and squeezes my hand.

"Evie, your dad's pretty scary. I'm sure death would shit himself if he has to try and take your dad from you." Rhett's words make me smile. "I know I would fight with everything I have to stay with you, and I'm not half as badass as he is."

I chuckle, "He is pretty badass."

"Tell me more about him. What does he do for a living? How did you find him?"

"Dad's a Navy SEAL."

Rhett's eyebrows shoot up. "Damn, Evie, I take back what I said. You have nothing to worry about. Your dad is the best of the best."

"He is?" I frown at myself when I hear how stupid the question sounds. "I mean, I know he is. I just don't understand all the military and Navy terms."

"Evie, your dad is trained to survive anything."

I smile at the comforting words, then whisper, "He searched for me, Rhett. He thought I was dead."

Rhett's mouth twitches at the corner. "But you found him, Evie. That's amazing."

"There was just something inside of me that wouldn't let me give up."

"After meeting your dad, I now understand where you get your strength from."

I frown at his words. "Dad says I'm like mom, that she wouldn't have given up either."

"You're a survivor, Evie, just like him. No matter what life throws at you, you get up, and you keep trying. I've always admired that most about you."

After meeting with Rhett, I catch a cab to take me to *Marilyn's*.

It was really nice seeing Rhett again. We talked about so many things. It's funny how I learned more about him in the last four hours than I did in the two years back when we were in school.

When the cab stops in front of the restaurant, my stomach tightens. I've been doing my best to avoid Kyle since he lost his temper and said all those cruel things to me. But it's time I face him.

I walk in the front entrance, and I feel eyes on me as I walk to the office in the back. I knock on the door, and when Kyle barks, "Come in!" I open it.

I see the surprise on his face because I'm here so early.

"Well, if it isn't Evie Cole, finally gracing me with her fucking presence."

I ignore his snide comment and walking to his desk, I take the envelope from my bag. I place it down in front of him.

"That's my resignation letter," I say, and the words feel freeing. "Also, it's over between us."

I turn to walk away when he darts up.

"You don't get to say when it's over between us," he hisses. He grabs my resignation letter and tears it in half. "I own you."

Anger starts to bubble in my chest. "You don't own me, Kyle. I'm not a piece of property."

He moves fast, stalking around his desk. I turn and rush to the door, scared of what he might do, but before I reach it, he grabs hold of my shoulders and slams me into the wall. He presses his body hard against my back, pinning me. Hissing in my ear, he says, "The day you opened your fucking legs, you became my property. You will do as I say until I decide otherwise. Do you fucking understand?"

I nod just so he'll let go of me. It works, and the second he steps back, I bring my elbow back with all my strength and slam it into his throat. Kyle makes a gagging sound as I rush out the door.

When I'm a safe distance away from him, I yell, "I'm not your property. Don't ever come near me again."

I run from the restaurant and quickly climb into a cab. Only once it's driving away from *Marilyn's* do I take a deep breath.

Chapter 32

Rhett

It's Miss Sebastian's birthday, and I think she invited half the world.

I'm excited to see Mia and Danny, and the others, of course. Mostly, I'm looking forward to spending time with Evie. This will be the first time we'll all be together, and that's pretty special in my books.

I knock on Evie's door, and anticipation rushes through me just at the thought of seeing her. We've only had a couple of coffee dates, getting to know each other.

I still can't believe my girl is into extreme sports. I've agreed to go bungee jumping with her soon. I'll probably shit myself, but for Evie, I'd jump off a bridge.

The door opens, and I'm once again struck by how happy she looks. My heart starts to beat faster when her smile doesn't falter.

"You're here," she says. In a flurry of movement, she crashes into my chest, and as her arms circle my waist, it feels as if my soul is taking a deep breath for the first time ever.

I wrap my arms around her before she has a chance to let go, and pressing my face into her hair, I fill my lungs with Evie's sweet scent.

"To what do I owe the hug?" I ask.

She grins up at me, and all I want to do is claim her mouth, carry her back into the apartment, and sink balls deep into her. I've never needed to be inside of a woman so much.

"I'm just happy to see you," she says, and before I can act on my desire, she rips free from me and barrels back into the apartment to grab her bag and a tray.

I glance down at the tray and ask, "You made Miss Sebastian unicorn cookies?"

"Yeah, Willow told me Miss Sebastian loves anything bedazzled."

Each one is decorated with a different color glitter.

"She's going to love it," I say as I pull her front door closed behind her. I lock it and shove the keys in my pocket. When she doesn't say anything about me keeping her keys, a slow smile spreads across my face.

"I'm so excited to see everyone," Evie says, almost bouncing next to me as we walk to my car.

"They can't wait either," I whisper as I open the passenger door for her.

On the drive over to Miss Sebastian's place, I try to prepare Evie for what to expect.

"Miss Sebastian hugs a lot, and she will probably say something to embarrass me. No, she'll definitely say something inappropriate. Just remember it's all coming from a good place."

A mischievous smile curves around Evie's lips. "Now, I really can't wait to meet her."

As we pull up to the house, I notice that almost everyone is here already. It looks like only Marcus and Willow still need to arrive.

I get out and jog around the car. Opening Evie's door, I take the tray from her so she can climb out. She straightens her black shirt that has the words *'You are bedazzlelicious'* printed over the front in purple glitter.

"Miss Sebastian is going to love your shirt," I mention. I don't add that I really love the way they show the curves of her tits.

"Willow made it," Evie says as she takes the tray back from me.

Before we can get close to the front door, it swings open, and Miss Sebastian comes rushing out.

"OhmyGod! You're here."

I grab the tray from Evie seconds before Miss Sebastian slams into her.

"My-chunk-of-hunk-finally-grew-a-pair-of-glitter-rocks. I'm so happy you could come. "I couldn't sleep last night. I just wanted to meet you already. "You're-so-pretty!"

Then Miss Sebastian pulls back, and she notices the shirt Evie is wearing.

"Oh-my-God! "Ahhhhhhhh! "I-love-your-shirt."

Evie's smile keeps growing, and when Miss Sebastian finally glances in my direction, the tray catches her eyes.

Her hands fly to her cheeks. "Ahhhhhhhhhhhhh. Bedazzled unicorns!"

She grabs the tray from me and holds the damn thing like a newborn baby, cooing at each fucking cookie.

"Yeah, no one will be getting near those," I grumble under my breath.

Miss Sebastian hears me and shoots me a glare that promises pain and destruction.

266

"Touch my bedazzled babies, and I'll show you my cray-cray side."

She twirls around on her heels, probably to go hide the tray so none of us can find it. As she disappears back into the house in a burst of color, I chuckle.

"And that's my Miss Sebastian in all her glory."

When I glance down at Evie, the look of wonder on her face catches me by surprise.

"What's that look for?"

She places a hand on my chest, and standing on her toes, she presses a kiss to my cheek. My hands instantly grab hold of her hips, and I have to fight the urge to yank her closer so I can feel her perfect body pressed against mine.

I've given her a couple of hugs since we met up again, but this is the first time I get to touch her. My fingers dig into her, and I realize all over again how small Evie is compared to me. She's always been tiny, but staring down at her and feeling her petite body under my hands just brings it home again.

As if it never entirely died, my protective side roars to life, knocking the breath from my lungs.

Before she pulls back, she whispers, "There's the Rhett I remember."

The words are my undoing, and I tug her closer. A surprised gasp parts her lips, and her eyes dart to mine.

As I start to lean down, my hands slide to the swells of her ass and gripping a handful of each cheek, I press her tightly to me until I feel her nipples straining against my chest.

The sound of a car pulling up the drive breaks the moment between us, and Evie almost stumbles in her hurry to pull back.

A deep blush colors her cheeks, and as she turns around to see who just got here, I use her body as a shield to shove my hard dick into a less visible position. I will it to calm down before I embarrass myself.

Willow rushes toward Evie, and they fall into an embrace.

Over the tops of their heads, I see Marcus. Looking at him now, I can't believe we almost lost him.

Marcus reaches a hand out to me, and I take hold of it and then yank him into a bear hug.

"You've gotta stop doing that, dude," he grumbles, but there's no sting to his words, and that's why I'll never stop.

"I'm just so damn happy to see you," I say as we pull apart the next second. Bro-code and all, we keep physical touching to a split-second max.

"You saw me yesterday," he says dryly.

"What can I say, I can't go a day without seeing your pretty face," I joke.

He shoots a glare at me. "I'm not pretty."

"Yes, you are, Pretty-Boy," Willow says as she hooks her arm into his.

Marcus just shakes his head, then he looks at Evie. I notice the slight movement as Evie scoots closer to me. There's a nervous look on her face as she starts to worry her bottom lip.

My eyes dart between Evie and Marcus, giving them a moment.

When Marcus moves forward, Willow lets go of his arm.

Evie takes a step back right before Marcus wraps her up in a hug.

"Oh," the word pops from her, and her green eyes grow huge as saucers. It takes her a minute to respond, and her movements are careful as she wraps her arms around Marcus' waist.

"I'm sorry I was such a bastard to you," he whispers.

Willow walks to me and taking my hand, she pulls me away from them so they'll have some privacy.

"He needs to do this," she whispers.

I strain my ears to hear what he's saying to Evie, and luckily Willow doesn't drag me too far away.

"Thank you for everything you've done for Willow. Thank you for being there for her when I wasn't. Especially during the surgery."

As she presses her cheek to his chest, I have a clear view of Evie's face. She shuts her eyes tightly as a smile curves around her full lips. "You're welcome."

When Marcus finally lets go of Evie, I step forward, and the second she's within my reach, I wrap my arm around her shoulders and pull her to my side. I feel her fingers grab hold of my shirt, and it makes a smile tug at the corner of my mouth. I don't let go of her as we walk through the house.

"Where's my birthday girl?" Marcus yells.

"Who's your girl? I'm a woman, darling. You should know, seeing as you paid for it," Miss Sebastian shrieks from the direction of the bedroom.

We hear her heels clicking rapidly on the tiles, and then she comes hurrying into the living room. Marcus opens his arms wide, just in time to catch her. Wrapping his arms around her, he lifts her feet off the floor, which makes Miss Sebastian shriek with laughter.

When he sets her back down, he frames her face and says, "Happy birthday, babe." He presses a firm kiss to her mouth.

"Who's the stranger fondling my wife?" Ryan shouts, a smile warming his face.

Marcus tucks Miss Sebastian in under his arm as he shakes Ryan's hand. "You better hold on tight to her. One of these days I'm going to steal her."

"Aww, you guys," Miss Sebastian gushes in her element with being the center of attention.

"You'll have to get in line, dude," I say, which has the desired effect on Miss Sebastian.

"You haven't even wished me a happy birthday yet!" She pulls free from Marcus' hold and stalks towards me.

"You didn't give me a chance," I argue. "Plus, you can't be upset with me. Look," I push Evie in front of me, handing her over as some kind of peace offering, "I brought you a new angel-girl. I get bonus points for the unicorn cookies she baked and the shirt she's wearing."

Instantly the scowl vanishes from Miss Sebastian's face, and she becomes a mother hen. Grabbing Evie's hand, she yanks her forward. "Meet my chunk of a hunk. Ryan, this is Rhett's happiness."

Evie's laughing by the time she gets to shake Ryan's hand.

Miss Sebastian is right, though. The woman with the flaming hair, wide green eyes, and heart of gold, is my happiness. It feels like it took forever to find her.

As everyone starts to move outdoors to where the rest of the gang is, I reach for Evie's hand and link our fingers.

"It's taken me a second to fall in love with Miss Sebastian, and a lifetime won't be enough to forget her," Evie murmurs.

Miss Sebastian stops dead in her tracks. When she turns around, her eyes are sparkling with tears. "Mother of all that's bedazzled, look what my angel-girl has gone and done." Her hand flitters in front of her eyes as she rapidly blinks. "I'm gonna cry, and even though I'm sexy as hell, my face becomes a nuclear disaster area when I cry."

Miss Sebastian opens her arms wide as she comes at us, and letting go of Evie's hand, I place an arm around her waist to help her brace for the impact.

Miss Sebastian crashes into us. When she's done hugging us, she stands on her toes and wrapping an arm around my neck, yanks me closer so she can reach my ear.

"This is the best birthday present. All I wanted was for you to be happy. Thank you for taking your handsome head out of that sexy ass of yours and for going after my angel-girl."

Chapter 33

Evie

Can a heart burst from too much happiness? Is there even such a thing as being too happy?

A year ago, I had nothing, and now... now I have everything I've ever dreamt about.

As Miss Sebastian dashes away from us, Rhett tightens his arm around my waist. He's never touched me so much before, and it keeps sending tingles racing through my body.

It feels surreal, being his sole focus. We had some moments back when we were in school, but the way he looks at me now, and he touches me... it's different.

Every touch feels like a promise of passion, and every look weakens my knees.

I'm the one who's been slowing down the pace between us, but now I'm no longer sure that's what I really want.

As we walk out onto the patio, I glance around.

"Carter!" Della shrieks as he tosses her over his shoulder. He starts to stalk towards the swimming pool, and a little girl jumps up and down with excitement near them.

"Don't you dare," Della hisses seconds before he throws her into the water, clothes and all.

"Yay," the little girl shrieks before she runs towards the water. Carter catches her in time, swinging her into the air.

"Not yet, Princess. You can't ruin your dress."

She pouts at him and crosses her tiny arms over her chest. "But, I wanna swim with Mommy."

"After we've eaten, you can change into your Little Mermaid bathing suit," he tries to negotiate with her.

Della swims to the edge and drags herself out.

"But Mommy's already getting out," the little girl argues.

"Don't worry, I'll throw her back in for you," Carter says with a mischievous grin.

At that moment, the little girl's eyes land on Rhett, and she lets out a squeal.

"Put me down. Hurry!" She wiggles until Carter sets her back on her feet.

Like a little bolt of lightning, she races over to us.

"Uncle Ledge," she cries, and she flings herself at him.

Rhett scoops her up and tosses her into the air before catching her again.

"That's a pretty dress you're wearing, Princess," he says as he plants a big kiss on her chubby cheek.

Her eyes zoom in on me, and again she starts to wiggle like a little worm until Rhett sets her down.

Her eyes are huge as she watches me, and curiosity makes her little face shine with wonder.

She crooks her tiny finger at me, showing for me to crouch down.

I sink down to my knees and smile at her. She places her hand against my cheek and whispers, "I've been waiting for for-eeeeeever to meet you."

My smile becomes wobbly, and I swallow hard on the lump in my throat.

"Hi, Princess Danny," I whisper once I can trust my voice to not fail me.

"Are you finished with your adventure?" she asks.

"Yeah," I breathe the word.

She glances up at Rhett and swallows hard. It looks like she's just been told Santa isn't real.

"What's wrong?" I ask as worry curls in my stomach. If Danny doesn't like me, I don't know what I'll do. She's Rhett's world.

Her bottom lip starts to tremble, and she whispers, "Daddy says it's good to share my things with others."

Not understanding, my eyes dart up to Rhett, hoping he can help. But his eyes are glued to Danny's face with such intensity it makes my heart stop.

This moment isn't about me.

I look back to Danny and patiently wait for her to continue. Her shoulders slump, and placing her hands behind her back, she digs the toe of her glittering flats into the ground.

"Uncle Ledge is my fairy-godfather," she whispers, "but it's okay if I have to share him with you."

"Oh, Danny," I whisper when I realize Danny is sad because she thinks I'll take Rhett from her.

I reach for her arm and pull it from behind her back. Her eyes keep jumping between my face and our hands as I uncurl her little fingers.

I reach up with my other hand, grab hold of Rhett's hand and yank him down. He crashes into me but catches himself in time before he squashes me.

I place Rhett's hand palm to palm against Danny's, and the sadness in her eyes makes space for curiosity.

"See how big Rhe... ah... Uncle Ledge's hand is?"

She nods eagerly.

I place my hand on the back of Danny's, and whisper, "See how much space is still left of Uncle Ledge's hand?"

"Yes," she breathes.

"It's the same with Uncle Ledge's heart. You're right in the center of it, and no matter who comes into his heart, there will always be extra space for them so you won't have to ever share the space you have."

A bright smile lights up her entire face.

"Phew." Using her other hand, she wipes at the imaginary beads of sweat on her forehead. "It's a lot of hard work to worry."

I chuckle as I let go of her hand and sit back.

Rhett presses a kiss to Danny's forehead. He whispers something in her ear, which makes her giggle. She nods excitedly before she waits for him to walk over to where Carter and Della are standing, watching me with their daughter.

"Aunty-Princess-Anna," Danny's voice yanks my attention back to her. She giggles as she says, "Uncle Ledge asks if he can be your Kristoff?"

For a moment, I have to wrack my memory to remember that Kristoff is Anna's love interest in *Frozen*.

My eyes widen, and my mouth drops open, which only makes Danny giggle more.

"Silly," Danny teases, "you have to say yes."

"Yes," the word is nothing but a burst of air, but it's enough for Danny because she twirls around before running to Rhett, yelling at the top of her lungs, "She said yes, Uncle Ledge. You have to kiss her now."

"You're right, Princess," Rhett says with a wicked gleam in his eyes.

I quickly scramble to my feet, not sure what to expect right now.

As his long legs eat up the distance between us, Danny shouts, "Not too long. That will be gross."

Rhett looks dangerously hot as he stalks right at me, his eyes locked on mine. His body collides with mine, his arm wraps around my waist, and tipping me backward, his mouth claims mine.

Even though he keeps the kiss PG-rated, Rhett becomes the sole focus of my entire universe as our mouths meet for the first time.

He pulls me back up and keeping his arm wrapped around my waist, he ends the kiss. When my eyes flutter open, they meet his heated ones.

"Took you long enough," I whisper, my voice hoarse from wanting this man.

A sexy grin tugs at the corner of his mouth, as he whispers, "I promise I'll make it up to you when we leave here."

Wow. Can we leave already?

As Rhett steps back, everyone starts to clap, making my cheeks flame up. Thankfully, they all have mercy on me and soon return to the various conversations they were having before Rhett, and I gave them a show.

The girls all rush over, each taking a turn to hug me. Della grips the towel around her with one hand, while she holds me with her free arm.

"Thank you," she whispers, and she doesn't need to say more. I know she's referring to the moment between her daughter and me.

Rhett brings me a soda while I catch up with the girls, and immediately Miss Sebastian's eyes grow wide.

"You're not having any wine? Is there a reason?" Her eyes drop to my stomach, and I swear I'm about to go up in flames with embarrassment.

"On no! No-no-no, it's nothing like that," I say quickly. "I'm not a big fan of alcohol."

Miss Sebastian seems to deflate right before our eyes. "A girl can dream," she whispers.

"Don't worry, Miss Sebastian," Rhett says as he throws an arm around my shoulders. "Soon enough you'll have a dozen of mini-me's running around."

Her face brightens with hope. "Just make sure you give your little chunks of hunks a map. I'm sure by now they've forgotten what an egg looks like."

I made the mistake of taking a sip of soda, and it spurts out as I laugh at Miss Sebastian's words. Wiping the drops from my chin with the back of my hand, I whisper, "I'm sorry. I didn't see that coming."

"Oh, honey, I don't blame you. My babykins took so long to go after you, I'm afraid the second his ding-dong sees your bejeweled land of fantasy, all those little chunks of hunks are going to take off like bedazzled rockets into outer space." She wags her manicured brows at me. "Instead of stars, I'm hoping he gives you fireworks."

For a full minute, I can only blink.

I can't believe we're talking about Rhett and I having sex.

"I might need that glass of wine now," I mutter to no one in particular.

"Thanks, Miss Sebastian," Rhett says as he pulls me away from the girls and towards the fire where all the guys are gathered. "On that note, I'm sure Evie is ready to run screaming for the hills."

"Don't you go sassing me, my babykins. Someone has to prepare my angel-girl," she calls out, making Rhett chuckle.

When we get to the guys, Jaxson and Logan smile at me, as they say at the same time, "Hi."

It makes me grin when they scowl at each other.

Jaxson gives me a quick hug. "I'm glad you're here."

Logan keeps his distance, though, and says, "Good to see you, Evie."

"Hey, guys. Thanks for having me," I say, feeling a little self-conscious as I dare a peek at Carter.

His face is so unyielding that I instantly drop my eyes to the ground. I guess he still doesn't like me.

"Rhett, do you mind if I borrow Evie for a second?" Carter asks, and I shut my eyes, praying Rhett says no.

"Sure."

My shoulders slump, and suddenly I wish Dad was here so I could hide behind him.

"Walk with me to the kitchen, Evie," Carter says. "I need to get the burgers and steaks."

I swallow hard as I follow him, wondering how on earth Danny is such a happy child when her dad is so scary.

By the time we reach the kitchen, I'm seriously thinking about making a run for the front door.

"It's none of my business," Carter says as he pins me with a daunting look, "but you know Rhett is very important to all of us."

I start to swallow repeatedly as my heart sinks into the shiny tiles at my feet. This is where Carter tells me I'm not good enough, that Rhett deserves more than what I can offer him.

"And I'm certain I'm speaking for everyone here, when I say," his mouth starts to pull into a smile, which confuses me, "thank you for giving Rhett's stubborn ass a second chance."

"Huh?" The word bursts from me, as I stare at Carter.

"For a while there, I was really concerned about Rhett. But now that he has you, I can finally relax. I'm glad you worked things out."

I still look like a gaping fish when he picks up a bowl of meat, places his hand on my shoulder, and gives it a light squeeze before leaving me alone in the kitchen.

I let out the breath I was holding.

Uhm… okay… I didn't expect that.

It's a relief to know Carter doesn't hate me.

Arms wrap around me from behind, and I know who it is without having to look.

"Are you okay?" Rhett whispers against my cheek.

I nod as I slowly turn around in his arms.

"Good, for a second there I thought you were going to climb over the counter so you could crawl away from Carter."

I slap his chest playfully. "It was one time! You're never going to let me forget, are you?"

Rhett shakes his head as his hands drop to my butt, and lifting my body against his, he walks us into a study. Using a foot, he nudges the door closed, then presses me up against the wall.

My stomach is alive with the buzzing of bees and fluttering of butterflies as he stares deep into my eyes.

"I knew I was done for when I saw you crawling toward the stairs," he whispers.

"Why?" I breathe the word, not wanting to ruin the moment between us.

"Let's just say the view was spectacular," he teases.

He starts to lower his head, and my eyes drop to his mouth.

An inch away, he stops and whispers, "I'm going to kiss you, Evie."

My eyes dart to his before dropping back to his lips. As I lift my chin to nod, his mouth crashes against mine.

My hands move from his shoulders, wrapping around the back of his neck as his fingers dig into my butt, and he lifts me higher so that I can wrap my legs around his waist.

When his tongue teases the seam of my mouth, I moan softly, opening for him. Feeling his tongue brush against mine, and tasting Rhett, sets off tiny explosions of pleasure all over my body.

Finally. Oh god, finally, I get to feel Rhett's mouth on mine.

Chapter 34

Rhett

After stealing that kiss from Evie in Miss Sebastian's study, all I can think about is being alone with her.

Pretending I wasn't being eaten alive by desire was one of the hardest things I've ever done. But I pulled it off, and as I'm walking Evie to her front door, I'm not sure I have the strength to say good night.

I remove her keys from my pocket and unlock her door.

A faint blush colors her cheeks, and she shyly looks up at me. The look alone is enough to bring me to my knees, but then she says, "I know it's late... but," she bites her bottom lip, and her eyes drop to my chest.

"But?" I ask, needing her to complete the sentence, more than I need my next breath.

"You're going to think it's too soon," her shoulders slump a little, "but I'd like it if you came in." Nervously, she tucks some curls behind her ears. "Stay the night," she whispers so softly that if my eyes weren't glued to her lips, I might not have heard them.

I take a step closer to her and placing a finger under her chin, I nudge her face up until our eyes meet.

"Are you sure?" I ask. "I can wait."

Fuck no, I can't! I'm dying here, and only Evie can save me.

I fight my need for her, wanting the moment to be right for both of us, not just me.

"I've been sure since I woke up to you humping my butt," she teases.

"If only you knew what I was dreaming about," I tease her back.

I take another step forward, and she matches me by taking one backward and into the apartment.

She grips hold of the door, and I step to the side so she can close it. I wait for her to lock it, but when she reaches for the light switch, I grab her hand to stop her.

"Leave it off," I whisper. Even though it's dark, I can still see Evie with the moonlight shining in through the window.

I pull her closer, and when we're standing toe to toe, I bring both my hands to her face. I brush my knuckles over her silky skin, savoring the feel of her.

"I want to touch every inch of you, Evie," I growl, unable to keep the desire I feel for her at bay much longer. The exhilaration coursing through my veins is unlike anything I've experienced before.

She doesn't move a muscle as her big eyes shine in the dark. "Touch me then."

"I won't be able to stop," I warn her, scared by the tension coiling in my chest and the hunger flooding my gut.

"I don't want you to stop."

My hands are actually shaking as I drop them to her shoulders, and brushing them down her arms, I savor how delicate she feels.

I've never been so anxious to be with someone before. My breaths speed up until I'm afraid I'm going to pass out from too much excitement and lack of oxygen.

She tilts her head and bringing a hand to my cheek, she whispers, "What's wrong?"

I try to slow my breaths by reminding myself that this is Evie. I love her. I've wanted this moment for so long. But as I remind myself of what Evie means to me, my heartbeat joins my breaths in a race to see who can kill me first.

I never thought I'd say the words, but yet it's the sound of my voice filling my ears. "The anticipation is a little overwhelming."

"Do you want to stop? I'll understand."

She's so gentle with me right now, it's breaking my heart. I close my eyes and admit the truth to her. "I've never been with someone I love. I'm not sure I know what to do."

Evie's quiet for a moment, and I wait to hear the words, as she calls me out for being a manwhore.

"Will you let me show you?"

My eyes open, and I stare at the amazing woman in front of me. Instead of telling me I'm full of shit, she once again sees the part of me, so few have seen.

The part that's terrified of giving myself entirely to another person. The part that only fucks, because making love to a woman will give her the power to destroy me. The part of me that's been dying to be saved, to be loved, to be wanted for who I am.

"Yes," I whisper, giving Evie access to all that I am.

The reckless fool who kept her at a distance. The careless joker who tried to convince himself he didn't need her. The heartless bastard who fucked everything with a pulse and didn't care what he was doing to the woman he claimed to love. The ruthless asshole who broke her heart and let her go. But most of all – the *shameful* man.

Taking hold of my hand, she leads me to her bedroom. This time I don't stop her from switching on the light. She kicks off her shoes and then kneels at my feet.

She unties the laces of my boots before pulling them off one at a time. When I'm barefoot, she stands up and taking hold of the hem of my shirt, she pushes it up my chest and over my head.

Dropping the shirt to the floor, I'm not prepared for the sensations leveling me as Evie presses a kiss to the center of my chest.

Her breaths are hot on my skin as she kisses her way to my collarbone. Placing her hands on my shoulders, she lightly brushes the tips of her fingers down my chest, making every muscle I have, ripple with pleasure.

I'm so captivated by Evie that my nerves settle enough for my desire to take back control.

I place my hands on Evie's hips, and as I begin to move them higher, I push her shirt up until she's free of it.

Her curls drop back against her creamy skin, and the contrast is so stark, it isn't conceivable that anything more exquisite than this woman exists.

My hand slips behind her back, and I unclasp her bra. Taking hold of the straps, I begin to pull them down her shoulders. I drop it to the floor as I drink in the soft swells and tight nipples, and suddenly, I can't wait to taste her. My mouth starts to water.

I unbutton her jeans, and as I pull down the zip, my eyes dart up to Evie's face to make sure she's still okay with this happening between us.

Seeing the tears glistening on her cheeks, my heart all but stops with the fear that I've done something wrong. I frame her face and lean closer.

"What's wrong?"

She shakes her head and sniffs. "It's the way you're looking at me. It makes me feel like I'm... more. I didn't know how much I needed it until I saw the look on your face."

"You're not more, Evie," I whisper as I press my forehead to hers. "You're everything."

Chapter 35

Evie

You're everything.

The words aren't even cold on his lips when I crush my mouth to his.

I've never been brave enough to initiate a kiss, but seeing the love in Rhett's eyes, gives me the strength to take what I want.

I unfasten his belt, and then my fingers grow impatient as I work the button lose. A frustrated groan ripples up my throat as I struggle with the zip. I want to see him naked, to touch and taste him. I've waited so long for this moment that I'm all out of patience.

Rhett's hands close over mine, and he breaks the kiss.

When our eyes meet, I don't know what he sees on my face, but it makes a low growl rumble through his chest.

His body slams into mine, a strong arm wraps around my waist, and then I'm thrown onto the bed. Rhett yanks my jeans down.

Pulling his wallet out of his back pocket, he removes a condom from it. He tosses the piece of leather on my nightstand, then takes off his jeans.

I quickly wiggle out of my panties while Rhett strips out of his boxers. I haven't been with many men, but Rhett's size is so impressive that I rub my thighs together just so I can feel some friction.

The movement catches his eye as he rolls the condom over his thick length.

Taking hold of my thighs, Rhett spreads my legs open before he crawls onto the bed. The sight makes my body hum with anticipation.

The look on his face is wild, as he growls, "I'll worship you in ten minutes. Right now, I can't go slow."

I chuckle, but it dies a quick death as his head dips low, and his mouth latches onto the bundle of nerves between my legs.

I let out a shriek of intense pleasure, and my body tries to crawl out from under him, but he grabs hold of my hips and yanks me right back to where he wants me.

"Rhett, it's too –" My breath slams into my throat and cuts my words right off as Rhett pushes a finger inside me while sucking hard on my clit.

My heels dig into the covers, and my hips lift off the bed as the world shatters into shards of pleasure and color.

My body is still jerking uncontrollably as Rhett positions himself at my entrance.

He waits for me to look at him, before he pushes an inch inside of me, groaning, "This is what I've wanted. Fuck, Evie. How's it possible that you're both my undoing and my saving grace?"

The stretching feeling of him pushing inside me, and his words almost have me losing my mind.

I push my body hard against him, and I let out a moan of approval as he turns onto his back and allows me to straddle him.

I crush my mouth to his, and satisfaction fills me as he kisses me back with the same passion.

Rhett's hands grab hold of my ass, his fingers digging in deep as I break the kiss. I wrap my hand around his thick shaft so I can lower myself onto him.

"Fuck, this better not be another wet dream," he groans, and as I take him inside me, sinking all the way to the hilt, he barely breathes as ecstasy washes over him.

I'm mesmerized by his reaction to me as I start to move. He allows me to set the pace, and I keep it slow and deep. When he grabs hold of my hips, I remove his hands and place them on my breasts, keeping mine over his.

"Fuck, babe," he growls, his voice tight. He grinds his teeth and starts to pull his hands from beneath mine, but I tighten my hold on him.

"Don't move your hands. I have zip ties in the kitchen, and I'm not afraid to use them."

I squeeze him with my inner walls as I move slower, relishing in the feel of him inside of me. I throw my head back as his hips lift off of the bed, and he tries to thrust deeper.

"Babe... babe..." Hearing the need as his body starts to tremble, I slam down against him as hard as I can and begin moving faster.

Rhett's fingers dig into my flesh, bordering on being painful.

"Evie," he grinds out as his body bows off the bed.

Every muscle in Rhett's body tenses as his lips part and a breath hisses from him. I feel him jerk inside of me, and I slow down, sensually grinding myself against him as my own orgasm shreds through me.

As I'm coming down from the pleasure, Rhett rips his hands from where I've been keeping them locked to my breasts. He grabs hold of my shoulders and yanking me down against his chest, he rolls me onto my back.

Covering every inch of me with his body, he buries his face in my neck as a cry shudders through him. I wrap my arms around him and press kisses to his shoulder and neck as my own tears warm my cheeks.

When he regains control of himself, he doesn't try to hide his tears from me, but lifts his head and kisses me.

Tasting our tears, I now understand what Rhett meant when he said I'm both his undoing and saving grace. I feel exactly the same.

When he breaks the kiss and stares down at me, he asks, "Where did that come from?"

I grin sheepishly as I say, "I told you I'm into extreme sports."

Chapter 36

Rhett

I've wasted so much time trying to fill the hole in my chest with meaningless sex. Turns out, it wasn't a hole. It's a slot where Evie fits in perfectly.

Tomorrow she's moving in with her dad. The three of us are having a *goodbye* dinner tonight. It was Evie's idea, and Hayden and I are just going along with it.

That's something I'm still getting used to – calling Evie's dad by his first name.

I smile when I park my car outside Evie's building and see Hayden and Evie getting out of his car. They notice me too and wait so I can catch up with them.

"Good, you're just in time," Evie says as she presses a quick kiss to my lips and shoves a bag into my arms.

She rushes into the building ahead of us, and before I can follow, Hayden says, "Hold up." He waits for

Evie to be out of hearing distance before he continues, "It's Evie's birthday in two weeks."

"Yeah, I wanted to ask if you've made plans."

"We come from different worlds, and it's time they meet. Your group of friends and my team. Evie deserves to have everyone celebrate her birthday with her."

"I can arrange that. What do –" A scream makes a chill race down my spine, and my eyes lock with Hayden's.

"Evie," he breathes as he breaks out into a sprint.

Halfway up the stairs, we can hear her screaming.

"Daddy!"

"Rhett!"

My heart is beating out of my chest by the time we reach her apartment. I don't know what I expected, but seeing Evie standing on the couch with a frying pan in her hands is definitely not it.

She glares at something on the other side of the couch and figuring it's a mouse, I move closer.

Hayden walks toward Evie as I rush to see what has her cornered.

"Daddy," she says as she drops the pan and throws her arms around him. She clings to him like a spider monkey, and as I get closer, the reason for Evie's strange behavior groans.

"I didn't know he was in here. He scared me, so I whacked him with the pan I was holding. Did I kill him?"

"Who the fuck are you?" I growl at the guy who's holding his hand to a bleeding spot on his head.

Hayden sets Evie down on her feet and growls, "Stay right here." He stalks around the couch and grabs hold of the guy's neck, hauling him into the air.

"Who is he?" Hayden asks Evie.

She shrugs and looking a little guilty she whispers, "A mistake. In my defense, I tried to fix the mistake once I knew better. I'm sorry, Daddy."

"That's alright."

I watch the interaction with fascination, not worried about the *mistake* that's being strangled by Hayden.

"Do me a favor?" Hayden waits for her to nod before he continues. "Go to your room and close the door." His eyes flick to the guy, and they turn hard with rage. "Daddy's going to take care of the mistake, and I don't want you to witness it."

We both watch Evie walk to her room. She glances at us from over her shoulder and mouths the word, "Sorry."

Before she closes the door, she says, "Don't kill him. I don't want to have to forfeit my deposit on this place because there are bloodstains on the carpet and walls."

"Evie. The door," Hayden says, giving her a pointed look.

"Yes, Daddy." She shuts it quickly.

I look back to the guy who's becoming more lucid after Evie knocked him senseless.

"Rhett," Hayden says, dropping the guy back onto the floor.

"Yeah."

"You want to learn a neat trick?" he asks as he crouches down by the guy's head.

"Sure."

The guy finally snaps out of the daze, Evie knocked him into and seeing Hayden's threatening face, his eyes widen.

"Grab a spoon from the kitchen," Hayden says, never taking his eyes from the guy.

I walk to the kitchen and open the drawer.

"You want the big spoon or little spoon?" I call back to him.

"Big spoon."

"That would've been my choice as well," I say as I bring the spoon back to Hayden and hand it to him.

The guy tries to sit up, but Hayden's hand slams into his throat and pins him back against the floor. With his free hand, he brings the spoon to the guy's left eye socket.

"What the fuck are you doing in my daughter's apartment?"

A garbled string of words flies out of the guy's mouth.

"Did you understand any of that?" Hayden asks.

I cross my arms over my chest. "Didn't make a lick of sense to me."

Hayden starts to apply pressure by pressing the spoon under the guy's eyelid.

"Dude, you better talk," I warn him.

"I used to date her," he screams. "Stop! Please stop. I just wanted to scare her. I wouldn't have hurt her."

"Your name," Hayden hisses.

"Kyle."

"Well, Kyle, today's your lucky day. Not only will I allow you to keep your eye, but I'll also call you a cab."

I frown at this.

"Can't we hurt him a little bit?" I ask, wanting to make him bleed for trying to attack Evie.

Hayden pulls the guy to his feet.

"Rhett, because I like you, I'll let you throw a few punches while I call the cab. How does that sound?"

"Like a deal, I can't pass up," I growl as I grab hold of Kyle, and the second Hayden steps back, my fist connects with Kyle's jaw.

Kyle's grunt makes Evie call out from behind the door. "No blood on my carpet!"

"Don't worry, babe," I yell back as I deliver another blow to the fucker's face, "I've got this!"

I'm disappointed when Kyle passes out after the third blow, and I let him drop to the floor.

Hayden shakes his head while staring down at Kyle.

"You've got a good, solid punch," he says.

"Thanks," I say, grinning at the compliment.

"Next time hit a little softer. Then you can torture them for longer."

"I'll remember that." I point to his phone. "Who did you call?"

"Cops. That reminds me." He rushes to the bedroom and opens the door, "You can come out now."

Evie comes out, and the second she sees the blood, her hands fly to her hips, and she scowls at me.

"You said you got this," she snaps.

"I do. I'll get a cleaning company out."

"Oh." She lets out a relieved sigh. Okay."

"Evie, when the cops get here, you'll need to give a statement. The basic thing we're all going with is that we walked in, the idiot attacked Evie, and after a fight broke out, we managed to subdue him."

When the police show up, Kyle is already conscious again. We each give our statements while they arrest him.

By the time things calm down and they haul Kyle out of the apartment, it's too late to start cooking dinner.

"I vote we order in," I say as I pick up the bag, I set down on the table earlier.

"I second that," Hayden says.

"I'm outvoted," Evie grins. "Not that I mind."

We order pizza, and while we're eating, we go over the details for the next day.

Chapter 37

Evie

Before I open the front door, I hear hushed voices on the other side.

"Smile," a man hisses. Then a second later, "Shit, no, don't smile. You'll scare her."

Doing my best to hold the laughter in, I open the door. Instantly, all four men straighten their backs and smile so broadly, all I see are teeth.

When I burst out laughing, the look on their faces become even funnier.

One of the men glances at the ones next to him, and grumbles, "I told you not to smile."

I manage to calm down enough so I can reach out a hand to the first man.

"I'm Evie."

A chorus of hi's sound up. The one shaking my hand says, "Thank God you didn't get your father's looks. I was a bit worried when he told us he found you."

Dad comes walking out of the kitchen. "I heard that." Then he adds, "The one with a death wish is Dave." Dad points at each of them. "Max, Axel, and Mike."

Dad throws his arm around my shoulders and says, "Team, this is my little girl."

I start to feel a little awkward when they all just stare at me.

Axel is the first to move as he pulls me away from Dad and into the living room.

"Let me tell you about your old man. We were stuck in a shit hole –"

"Watch your language!" Dad snaps.

Axel rolls his eyes, but continues, "We were stuck in a poop hole. I mean an *actual* poop hole. We figured it would be the last place anyone would search for us. Luckily, I wasn't stuck at the bottom."

"Nope, that would've been me," Dave says dryly.

I listen to them bantering while I take my time to look at each of the men.

Mike can't be much older than me. He's attractive in a boyish kind of way, but the second you look into his eyes, the boy fades to the background, and I see the same inner strength that Dad has.

Max could be in his thirties, it's hard to tell. His light brown hair is shaved short, and his brown eyes never stop moving.

Axel looks like a big teddy bear with his thick beard.

Dave stands next to Dad, and I get a feeling they're really close even though Dave is much younger than Dad.

I've heard so much about them and have been looking forward to meeting the men who seem to be like brothers to my father.

"Let's get going," Dad says. Actually, it's more like an order. "I promised my girl fun."

Only then does Dad glance around the apartment. "Where's Rhett?"

At that moment, Rhett comes out of the bathroom.

"I was worried there for a second. Thought you made a run for it," Dad taunts Rhett as he throws his arm over Rhett's shoulder. "Team, this is my soon-to-be son-in-law."

I cover my mouth when the proud look on Dad's face makes my eyes burn.

"Yeah-yeah," Axel growls. "You're gonna make *our* girl cry on her birthday."

That seems to remind everyone why they're here, and a chorus of *happy birthdays* sounds up.

Axel holds me tight as he gets up, pulling me to my feet.

"*Our* girl?" Dad asks, trying to hide the smile, threatening to break over his face.

"We share rations and ammo, it's only right that we share the kids as well," Axel says.

The other guys nod in agreement, effectively out voting Dad.

On the way to the secret destination, I can't contain my happiness and excitement.

Dad sneaked Rhett into the apartment while I was still asleep. They woke me singing happy birthday and didn't even give me time to pull a brush through my hair before I had to open a mountain of presents.

My eyes begin to burn with unshed tears when I think of the letters Dad gave me. They were the ones Mom wrote to him while she was pregnant with me.

I placed them under my pillow. I'll read them tonight when I'm alone.

When we get to the destination, I'm surprised to see Carter, Logan, Jaxson, Marcus, and Ryan here as well.

"Hey guys, where are the women?" I ask once I'm out of the car.

"Once Leigh explained in detail what the chances are of someone falling to their death, they all chickened out," Jaxson answers.

"Fall?" I frown, and then Rhett points to a huge sign I somehow missed. "We're going bungee jumping?" I shriek.

"You know, guys," Marcus says as he places his hand over his heart, "With my heart and all –"

"Shut it. Leigh cleared you. If I'm jumping, you're jumping." Jaxson stops him from backing out.

"Logan, are my affairs in order?" Carter whispers.

"Yep. Don't even think about backing out now. You dragged me here," Logan mumbles back.

I chuckle as I ask Ryan, "You're jumping?"

"I had a choice between jumping or staying with the women. You bet your sweet behind I'm jumping."

Dad laughs, and he quickly introduces the two groups of men to each other.

When we're all schooled adequately on the jumping rules, Dad and Carter go first.

309

When they fall forward, their whoops and shouts echo around us.

Axel jumps with Logan, then Mike and Jaxson go, followed by Dave and Marcus. Max and Ryan get ready to go next when Rhett pulls me to the side.

"Please don't think less of me when I scream like a girl on the way down," he whispers.

"I won't, and I've heard you scream. You don't sound like a girl. Trust me," I whisper back.

"I do," he says, staring deep into my eyes.

"You do what?" I ask a little confused.

"I trust you, Evie."

"Evie, Rhett, you're up," Dad calls out before I can respond to the enormous bomb Rhett just dropped on me.

When I start to walk toward the left jumping podium, Dad calls out, "No, Evie. You're jumping tandem with Rhett."

"But, Dad," I start to argue.

"For Rhett's sake," he yells.

"Oh, sure," I say, changing my mind in a split-second which makes Dad and the others laugh.

They strap us in, and as we move to the edge of the podium, Rhett's arms tighten around me.

"It's going to be fun," I say as I start to lean to the side.

"Evie." The urgency in Rhett's voice grabs my full attention, but it's too late to stop from jumping as we fall over the side. "Maaaaaaaarryyyyyyyy meeeeeeee," Rhett screams all the way down.

When I finally catch my breath, and we're swinging from side to side, I press my mouth to Rhett's and kiss him with everything I feel at the moment.

When the cord jerks, Rhett breaks the kiss, and breathlessly asks, "Will you marry me?"

"Rhett Daniels, you sure know how to make a girl weak in the knees." I wrap my arms around his neck and whisper in his ear, "Yes."

He hollers so loudly, I press my ear against his chest, so I don't lose my hearing.

When the guys up on the bridge, hear Rhett's crazy hollering, one of them shouts, "She said yes."

Dear Hayden,

I miss you so much. I can't believe you've been gone for eight months already. You're going to want to reconsider marrying me when you see me again. I'm huge!

I have a surprise for you. Our little bean finally decided to show us what SHE is. Yes! We're having a daughter.

I hope she has your eyes. God, I miss your eyes most.

I can't wait for you to come home so we can get married and be a family. Just you, me, and our darling daughter.

Please keep yourself safe. Our daughter is going to need you.

We love you, Hayden.

Your Joey & Little Bean.

Reading my mom's words make me feel so much closer to her. She was excited to have me, and that makes all the difference in the world.

Chapter 38

Rhett

It's the first weekend Evie is spending at my place since we got engaged. I was just about to do something drastic, like kidnap her.

Yeah, right. Hayden would kill you.

I have the front door open, and when I hear her approaching, I rush out the door.

"Hi," she says with a huge smile, which turns into laughter when I throw her over my shoulder and stalk back to the apartment.

"My bag! I dropped it," she laughs.

I turn around, grab the bag and rush through the door, kicking it shut behind us. Dropping the bag right there, I walk to my bedroom and only stop when I toss Evie on the bed.

A chuckle escapes her every now and then as I strip her naked before getting rid of my clothes.

As I reach for the nightstand drawer to grab a condom, Evie says, "Oh, we're safe now. I've been on the pill long enough."

"Babe, that's the best news I've had all week," I growl as I crawl over her body. I press a quick kiss to her lips. "Hi. I missed you. I'm going to fuck you this entire weekend."

She laughs as I kiss my way down her body, and when I suck her clit into my mouth, it fizzles into a moan.

I only give her pussy enough attention to get her wet before crawling back up her body. Taking hold of her hands, I push them over her head.

"Feel the bars?" I ask, and as she takes hold of them, I say, "Don't let go of them."

"Okay," she whispers.

"Now that I have you exactly where I want you," I whisper as I take hold of her hips and turn her onto her stomach, "I can finally have my wicked way with this ass."

"What?" she shrieks as she glances over her shoulder at me.

"Trust me, babe. I won't hurt you."

314

Straddling her thighs, I squirt some baby oil into the palm of my hand. I start to rub it all over her back before I take my time touching every inch of skin.

I scoot down and massage the swells of her ass, and when I slip my hand in between her legs, I can feel how ready she is. Taking a pillow, I place it under her abdomen, so her ass is in the air, and I slowly massage her opening until she starts pushing up, trying to get me to move back to her pussy.

When I caress every intimate part of her except for her pussy, she starts to whimper in frustration.

I lean over and whisper in her ear, "When I sink my cock deep into your pussy, you're going to come immediately."

"Rhett," she breathes as her hips start to swivel in need.

Taking the blindfold from the drawer, I work gently as I tie it over her eyes, so I don't catch her hair by accident.

When I'm sure she can't see a thing, I press my chest against her back and softly bite her shoulder. My fingers trail down her ass and finding her opening, I caress her until her body pushes back against mine.

I nibble on her earlobe and whisper, "Have you ever done it from behind?"

"No."

"Can I?" I ask.

She nods as she bites her bottom lip. She's nervous, which is understandable.

"I love your ass so much, Evie. The first time I saw you bending over a couch, I fell so hard for your ass." Pushing the tip of my finger inside, I continue to whisper, "Remember that night you were crawling across the living room floor."

When she nods, I sit back between her legs and lifting her hips from the pillow, I move my thighs in under her. I position my cock at the entrance to her wet pussy, and as I start to push inside of her, my hands return to her ass.

Fucking hell, she feels good without a condom.

Once I'm seated inside of her, I keep still and watch as my fingers dig into her skin. I'll never get enough of Evie's body.

"My shirt was too big for you, and as you were crawling away, I had a perfect view of your tits swaying with every movement you made."

I circle the bundle of nerves at her ass before I push a finger inside. Evie's body jerks and her pussy squeezes my cock, which makes me slowly start a rhythm of finger fucking her ass.

"That night, I dreamt of fucking you. Just like we did our first time together." Pressing my finger deep inside of her, I keep it there as I reach under her with my other hand and pay attention to her clit.

"Rhett," she whimpers as she presses her ass hard into my hand and grinds her pussy on my cock. "I feel you everywhere."

"Almost," I whisper as I remove my hand from her clit, and slide it up her side. Covering her breast, I dig my fingers into her soft flesh until she grinds back against me, telling me that she loves the pressure.

Pulling my cock out of her, I slowly thrust back, mimicking the action with my finger in her ass.

"Ah... Rhett," she moans. Her body tenses until it sounds like she's wailing, and only then do I slam into her so hard I swear I see stars explode. I let go of her breast and pulling away from her, I grab hold of her hips and turn her back around.

Her breasts rise and fall with her quick breaths. I plunge my cock back into her pussy. Crushing my mouth to hers, I devour her. I thrust harder and faster, and when I feel my balls tightening as her body starts to tremble, I slam into her as I let go. Evie cries into my mouth when I empty myself inside of her.

Once we come down from our orgasms, I don't pull out, but keep thrusting slowly as I cover her body with mine. I place my arms on either side of her head, shove the blindfold off her face, and stare into her eyes.

She lets go of the bars and bring her hands to my face. With the tip of her finger, she caresses the curve of my lips.

"Can we have a little bean someday," she whispers.

"Little bean?" I ask.

"Yeah, that's what my mom called me while she was pregnant with me."

I never thought of having my own children. But the longer I stare into her eyes, the more I want a house full of red-curled, green-eyed little girls.

"Babe, when you're ready, just stop the pill, and we can have all the little beans you want."

Her smile warms her entire face, and I start to thrust deeper and keeping my eyes locked on the woman I love, I make love to her.

Epilogue

Rhett

Ten years later.

I glare at Carter until he finally gives up and looks at me.

"I'm not happy about this either," he snaps. "Go glare at Della. She's the one who said yes."

"You're Danny's father," I say. "You should've put your foot down."

"Oh yeah? The same way you put your foot down when Evie allowed Jade to have a sleepover, and she ended up inviting a boy?"

Did he have to remind me?

"Fuck, that night I didn't sleep at all. Trust my kid to have a boy for a best friend." I smile at Carter. "We should have chastity belts made for our girls. Miss Sebastian can bedazzle them."

"I can bedazzle what?" Miss Sebastian asks as she walks into the living room.

"Chastity belts," I say, and when Miss Sebastian's brow furrows, I add, "For our girls. You know, to protect them from all the little ding-dongs out there."

Miss Sebastian shoves her fists into her sides and glares at each of us.

"Now listen here, my chunks of hunks. My little princess is excited, and I will not have you ruin her first prom. You're all gonna behave, or I'll have your ding-dongs in a bedazzled vise before this night is over."

As if on cue, we all cross our legs to protect our manhoods from a bloodthirsty Miss Sebastian.

"Good. I'm glad we got that sorted." She looks at us expectantly, then frowns. "I swear, the older my chunks of hunks get, the less common sense you have. Does it take more brainpower to keep your ding-dongs working?"

"Did you have too much wine?" Marcus asks her.

Miss Sebastian gives him a glare that could have him shooting up daisies from ten feet under.

"Darling, don't go pushing my buttons. I'll switch to bitch mode before you can make a run for the door."

Marcus glances at me and pretending to cough, we all try to hide our smiles behind our hands.

"Get your sexy asses up!" She shrieks. "She's ready and waiting to come down the stairs."

"Why the hell didn't you say so in the first place?" Carter growls as he darts out of the chair.

We all rush after him and form a half-circle at the foot of the stairs.

"Princess?" Carter calls when there's no sign of Danny.

The next moment we only see a pair of bright blue eyes peeking at us from behind the wall.

"Are you all ready? I'm only doing this once," Danny calls out.

Yeah, she takes after her father.

"They're ready, Princess," Miss Sebastian calls out.

When Jaxson's phone starts to ring, and he reaches for it, Miss Sebastian slaps him upside the head.

"Don't even think about answering that call," she hisses.

Rubbing the back of his head, he whispers, "I wasn't going to. I was turning the damn thing to silent."

Miss Sebastian instantly relaxes. "Oh, okay."

We all stare at the top of the stairs, and when Danny walks out from behind the wall, the responses are instant.

"You're not leaving the house dressed like that!" Carter yells.

"Where's the rest of it?" I ask, praying this is a joke.

"You let her get dressed like that? What were you thinking?" Marcus turns to Miss Sebastian.

"I was thinking she's sixteen and going to her first prom," Miss Sebastian quickly defends Danny's choice of prom dress.

"Exactly," Logan snaps. "She's sixteen!"

"You're fucking with us, right?" Jaxson asks.

"F-Bomb!" Jamie, Della's little sister, yells. "That will be one hundred bucks, Jax." She smiles at Danny. "Thanks, I owe you one. Now I have money for gas." Then she holds her hand out to Jaxson, who begrudgingly pays up. Jamie shrugs as she takes it with a smile. "End of month finances and all."

When Jamie rushes out the door, I know it's because she wants to avoid the shit storm that's about to hit this house, as we all turn back to Danny.

Her beautiful face looks heartbroken as her chin starts to tremble.

"I knew you wouldn't like it," she mumbles.

"Princess," Carter coos as he climbs the stairs, "You look beautiful. It's just that there's way too much skin showing. What happened to that gown you got?"

Danny rolls her eyes. "This is the gown, Daddy. Aunty Willow just made some minor adjustments."

"Willow!" Marcus yells.

Willow comes rushing in but stops when she sees all of our faces.

"Did you leave your glasses at home?" Marcus asks.

Willow's eyes widen and then she lets him have it.

"Marcus Reed, I will slap you so hard you'll see stars for days. Don't you talk to me like that!"

The next second, Miss Sebastian slaps Marcus upside the head.

"All taken care of, my angel-girl," she calls out sweetly.

"Guys!" I snap. "Can we focus on the fact that Danny is only wearing half a dress?"

"Uncle Ledge," Danny says, and hearing the tearful way she's saying my name instantly makes me feel like shit.

"Princess, it hardly covers your shoulders," I try to explain. "Where are the sleeves?"

323

"That's it!" Della snaps as she comes up behind Danny. "All of you in the living room now!"

"Oh, shit," I mumble as we all sheepishly trudge back to the living room with Della right behind us.

"Sit," she snaps, and like one man, we all plop down, with the same dreaded look on our faces. "Enough is enough! Danny has been looking forward to this night for weeks. There's nothing wrong with the dress she's wearing."

She glances over her shoulder to where Danny is standing, and her face softens a little as she says, "Baby, let Miss Sebastian touch up your makeup. Mommy doesn't want you to hear the next part."

"Fuck," Marcus groans as Della turns back to us.

"Just because you were the Screw Crew once, doesn't mean every single boy out there will be assholes like you. Reed is a nice boy."

"Reed is a fucking man with a working dick!" Carter growls. "He's a senior. My baby is a junior. I know what happens at proms."

"Carter Hayes, I will throat punch you. Danny and Reed have been dating for a year. That boy has always treated our daughter like the princess she is. He's too damn terrified of the bunch of you to treat her as anything less."

"That's true," I whisper. "I might have gone a little heavy on the threats."

"Danny looks beautiful, and unless you want me going psycho on you all, you will smile and tell her so. She's sixteen! She's a young woman. Treat her like one."

We all mumble our unhappiness with the situation, but none of us want to see Della in psycho mode.

"Now, get your asses to the bottom of the stairs and give Danny the attention she deserves."

We all walk back to the bottom of the stairs and form a half-circle.

"Smile," Della snaps. "Danny, you can come out," she calls up the stairs.

All you see are a bunch of men and a row of teeth as Danny once again steps out onto the landing.

"You look beautiful, Princess," Carter praises her.

I can feel Della's scowl burning into the side of my head.

"You're a vision, Princess," I say.

"I am?" Danny asks. "You're not just saying that because Mom is standing right behind you, and giving

325

you the same look I get when she catches me sneaking out of the house?"

"That look is pretty intense, right?"

"Yeah," Danny laughs.

I climb the stairs and raise my hand to her face, gently brushing a knuckle over the curve of her cheek.

"Daniele," I say. She knows I only call her by her given name if I'm dead serious. "I'll always see you as my little princess, who made me watch *Frozen* and sing *Let It Go* a million times. Whether it's tonight, or in ten years, I'm your fairy-godfather."

"Uncle Ledge," she breathes as she fights to hold back the tears.

"You are an absolute vision, Princess. Reed is lucky to have you as his prom date."

Just then, the doorbell rings.

"I'll get it while you finish with your uncles," I say as I rush to get to the door first.

I yank it open, and when Reed sees that it's me, he straightens his spine and swallows.

"Hi, Mr. Daniels."

"Reed," I say, and I don't move out of the way so he can come inside. "Before I let you near my princess, let's go over what will happen to you if you don't bring her back in one piece."

"Yes, Sir," Reed says. He sucks in a deep breath. "You will find me, and you will attach weights to my ding-dong before tossing me into the ocean."

"Good. What are the rules?" I ask.

"No drinking. No leaving her side at any time. No touching her below the neck. If there's a situation, I tell Danny to run and let them kill me because if anything happens to Danny, you'll kill me."

"Now that we have that out of the way," I say smiling, "come inside." Over my shoulder, I yell, "Danny, Reed's here."

Reed steps into the house as Danny comes walking into the foyer with Carter and the guys right behind her. I know the boy only has eyes for her when he doesn't even see the guys, but instead, just focuses on Danny.

"Wow," he breathes, "you look amazing."

"Thanks," Danny whispers with a blush on her cheeks. She steps forward and takes hold of Reed's hand, leaning her head on his shoulder. "Let's take photos so we can go, or we'll be late."

Watching my little girl smiling up at Reed while Della and Miss Sebastian take a dozen photos each, I realize she's changing into a beautiful woman.

I turn around as emotions swamp me, and walk out the front door before anyone can notice. At least, that's what I think until Danny calls after me. "Uncle Ledge, wait up!"

I stop and watch as she walks toward me. When she's standing in front of me, she asks, "You're leaving without saying goodbye?"

I shake my head. "No, princess. I'm just getting some fresh air."

She's always had an uncanny ability to know what I'm thinking and feeling.

Taking hold of my hand in both of hers, she takes a step forward.

"Uncle Ledge, no one will ever be able to replace you in my life. Every time I've felt like a princess, it was because of you. You've taught me I should never settle for a man who treats me as anything less."

I smile as I swallow back the tears, and pressing a kiss to her temple, I whisper, "I love you, Princess. Have fun at the ball."

"Love you now and always, Uncle Ledge," she whispers as she lets go of my hand and wraps her arms around my waist.

I hold her close, and as I close my eyes, I whisper, "Now and always, Princess."

∞∞∞∞

Five years later.

"Little Bean," I yell, so my voice will carry to the house.

"You called, Daddy?" Jade says. She comes over to where I'm standing in front of the flower bed.

"Yeah," I say, glancing at my daughter. "Come stand here by me." I hold my hand out to her.

She links our fingers together and stares up at my face, waiting to hear why I called her.

Jade got Evie's red curls, but my dark eyes. She's just turned fourteen. My heart constricts every time I notice how she looks less like my little bean, and more like a young woman.

"Keep your eye on the flowers," I say, turning my gaze back to the garden.

We wait a while in silence, then Jade whispers, "What are we waiting for?"

"You'll see in a second."

Finally, the little bird makes its appearance, its wings flapping so fast all we see is a blur.

"Aww…" Jade whispers.

We keep still as we watch the hummingbird gather spiderwebs before flying back to a nearby tree.

"Why did she take the spiderweb?" Jade asks.

"She's building a nest. Soon we'll have teeny, tiny hummingbirds. I looked up the meaning when I first saw one. Did you know their wings create the infinity symbol when in flight?"

"No, but it's awesome," Jade replies.

"Yeah, your Aunt Leigh will like that fact. Tell her next time you see her."

Getting to the reason I called my daughter out here, I get down on one knee in front of her and open my right hand. The promise ring I got Jade looks tiny where it's lying on my palm.

"Daddy," she gasps, covering her mouth with both her hands.

"Little Bean, you represent everything good I've done. I'm giving you this ring, so it will remind you no matter where you are or what you're doing, all you need to do is call, and I'll come running."

I take Jade's right hand and push the silver band onto her finger. It's an exact replica of the ring Evie wears.

"I promise to always be right behind you, Jade. So I can catch you when you fall, and hold you up when life gets hard. So I can cheer for you when you're happy, and help fix your mistakes when you make them. I'll always be right behind you because you come first in my life."

I wipe the tear from her cheek as she gives me a wobbly smile.

"I love you, Daddy," she whispers, wrapping her arms around my neck.

"I love you more, Little Bean."

More than anything because my daughter is my everything.

The End

Hayden & his team's story continues in False Perceptions, as well as Rhett & Evie's wedding.

Trinity Academy

Enemies To Lovers

Heartless
Novel #1
Carter Hayes & Della Truman

Reckless
Novel #2
Logan West & Mia Daniels

Careless
Novel #3
Jaxson West & Leigh Baxter

Ruthless
Novel #4
Marcus Reed & Willow Brooks

Shameless
Novel #5
Rhett Daniels & Evie Cole

False Perceptions
Novel #6
A Stand Alone Novel
Hayden Cole *(Evie's Dad)*

The Next Generation

COMING 2020

<u>HUNTER</u>
Novel #1
Hunter Chargill (*Mason and Kingsley's son*)
&
Jade Daniels (*Rhett & Evie's daughter*)

<u>KAO</u>
Novel #2
Kao Reed (*Marcus and Willow's son*)
&
Fallon Reyes (*Falcon & Layla's daughter*)

<u>NOAH</u>
Novel #3
Noah West (*Jaxson & Leigh's son*)
&
Carla Reyes (*Julian & Jamie's daughter*)

<u>RIKER</u>
Novel #4
Ryker West (*Logan & Mia's son*)
&
Danny Hayes (*Carter & Della's daughter*)

CHRISTOPHER
Novel #5
Christopher Hayes – (*Carter & Della's son*)
&
Dash West – (*Jaxson & Leigh's daughter*)

FOREST
Novel #6
Forest Hayes (*Carter & Della's son*)
&
Aria Chargill (*Mason & Kingsley's daughter*)

TRISTAN
Novel #7
Tristan Hayes – (*Carter & Della's son*)
&
Hana Cutler – (*Lake & Lee's daughter*)

JASE
Novel #8
Jase – (*Julian & Jamie's son*)
&
Mila – (*Logan & Mia's Daughter*)

Connect with me

Newsletter

FaceBook

Amazon

GoodReads

BookBub

Instagram

Twitter

Website

About the author

Michelle Heard is a Bestselling Romance Author who loves creating stories her readers can get lost in. She loves an alpha hero who is not afraid to fight for his woman.

Want to be up to date with what's happening in Michelle's world? Sign up to receive the latest news on her alpha hero releases → NEWSLETTER

If you enjoyed this book or any book, please consider leaving a review. It's appreciated by authors.

Acknowledgments

Sheldon, you hold my heart in your hands. Thank you for being the best son a mother can ask for.

To my beta readers, Morgan, Kelly, Kristine, Laura, and Leeann - thank you for being the godparents of my paperbaby.

A special thank you to every blogger and reader that took the time to take part in the cover reveal and release day.

Love ya all tons ;)